BIS BROWN

TALENT DISCOVERED

Sheridan Wittig

NEWMAN SPRINGS PUBLISHING
320 Broad Street
Red Bank, NJ 07701

First originally published by Newman Springs Publishing 2021

ISBN 978-1-63692-408-3 (Paperback)
ISBN 978-1-63692-409-0 (Digital)

Printed in the United States of America

Mary Michele Michael Maria Margaret Hinke Hearst —
You're the best friend ever!

♥ Sheridan

To Julia, you started this with me, and I am so grateful! Thank you for the support, the feedback, and making me feel like I was "good enough" to give it a shot! To my cousin Dana, thanks for loaning me the name! To my son Taylor, thank you for being honest when you read it and asking the hard questions. You helped make this book better! To my daughter Melody, thank you for your constant words of encouragement and excitement for me in this process. It's been a blast to share with you. To my daughter Lydia, you have always thought this was a good idea, and I'm so pleased you were right! Mom and Daddy, you always support me.

God surely had a plan.
Douglas, my love, thank you the most.

CHAPTER 1

SHADOWS AND MEMORIES

"Bishop, don't forget! This is important! Remember this. Don't forget! It will be a long time before you need this, but it's very important that you don't forget!"

Bishop was frightened. The man was very big, dark, and had his hand on Bishop's leg. His grip was strong; his eyes were forceful and intense.

"Please, Bishop, don't forget! Look at this box. Look at it! It has everything you'll need."

The man closed his eyes. Bishop looked at the box. It was as big as his chest. It was brown, and it had a top that opened like a flip-up box. Inside was fuzzy, like there was stuff in there, but he couldn't tell what. When Bishop finished looking at the box, he looked back at the man.

The man smiled. "Good, Bishop, you will need this one day. Remember."

As Bishop woke up, his head hurt—again. He kept having the same dream. Not every night, but often. Sometimes it would happen several times in a week, and sometimes it would be a month or two before he dreamed it. In between those dreams were other strange and very cool dreams. Sometimes Bishop could fly. Sometimes he could speak to animals, and sometimes he just knew what was going on around him. It was like he was walking around a television show that he had already seen.

"Bishop, get up! I've called you twice! I might be your mom, but I am most certainly not your alarm clock!"

Bishop's mom was quite happy to help with many things, but getting him up in the morning was not in her job description. She had bought him an alarm clock when he started kindergarten. She had told him it was part of the school supplies and all the big boys used them. He was quite surprised to figure out in fifth grade that she had not been exactly truthful about that. She laughed when he told her that it wasn't part of the school supplies. She said that at the Brown household, it was!

Breakfast was pretty normal that morning: cold cereal, cold juice, and everyone with their own book. Breakfast was quiet, quick, and usually done with little or no talking. This morning, however, was an exception.

"Mom, I keep having weird dreams. Lots of times, it's the same dream. Does that mean anything?" Bishop looked at his mom while he waited for a response.

His mom didn't look like she heard for just a minute, and Bishop wasn't surprised. She'd be finishing her sentence, paragraph, or chapter before she responded. It was okay; it was normal.

When she did look up, she had a funny look on her face. "What have you been dreaming, Little?"

Little was her nickname for Bishop when he was, well, little.

"I keep dreaming that I can fly, that I can talk to animals. Stuff like that."

His mom grinned. "Well, Little, sorry to disappoint you, but I don't think our nonexistent animals are listening to you. And if you could fly—well, that Frisbee on the roof a few weeks back would not have been a problem!"

"I have another dream too, Mom," Bishop said. "In that dream, there's this old man, and he keeps telling me to look at a box or something. I can't ever remember all the details. The box is big, and the man is really—I don't know—really intense maybe."

Bishop laughed at himself. He looked up at his mom; she was usually the first one to join in if someone were going to laugh at themself. She looked at him like his hair was sticking straight out from his head and bright purple.

"Really?" she asked. "Hmm. Would you recognize the man if you saw him?"

Recognize him if I saw him? Bishop was about to start laughing. What kind of science fiction was his mom reading! It had been a dream. Of course, Bishop's mom asked all kinds of weird questions sometimes, so he simply answered truthfully.

"Yes."

"Cool," his mom said and went back to her breakfast.

Several days went by, and his dreams repeated themselves. He spoke with animals. He flew, and he was told to remember. Then something really strange happened. When he got home from school, his mom called him over to the couch.

"Got homework?" she asked.

"Nope. I had some math homework, but I finished it in home-room. So I'm good to go!" Bishop said.

"Have a seat, Little. I wanted to show you some pictures from when you were young."

Bishop sat down, and his first thought was whether or not this was going to take long. He might not have homework, but he had no plans to sit on the couch and look at pictures of relatives and him running around in diapers. In fact, they almost never looked at pictures. Several were framed around the house, but there were no photo albums out—none in the bookshelves and none anywhere that Bishop knew of in the entire house. Mom had one now, but where had it come from?

Looking through the first pages of the book was hysterical: His mom and dad with big poofy hair, funny-looking glasses, and clothes that may have been in style back in the day but certainly weren't now—the list went on and on! His cousins, aunts, and uncles all wearing goofy stuff and sitting in an unfamiliar house.

Mom was telling him about the pictures that were taken that Thanksgiving. "This is your cousin Ruth. She was not around much, but you sat with her every chance you got. She refused to change your diaper though. She was so glad this Thanksgiving—you were potty trained! Do you remember Ruth?"

Bishop didn't remember Ruth, nor were many of the other faces familiar. A couple of the aunts and uncles and a couple of cousins, but that was it. There had to be forty people at this house, and most of them he had no idea who they were.

"I don't remember many of these people," he said.

Then Mom turned the page.

There was a woman in a flower-printed dress. She was not a tiny woman. She was short, yes; but she was round, happy, and familiar. Bishop looked at the picture for several seconds.

Then he said, "That's G-Ma Grace, isn't it?"

"Yes," his mother said. "She was my mother. She was very smart, pretty, and fun. She died soon after this. There was a car accident, and we lost her."

Bishop looked at her again. How could someone look so familiar if they had been gone since he was so little? Bishop looked at her picture some more.

Maybe it was because she was Mom's mother, he thought. *Maybe it's that whole genetic thing, and she just looks so much like Mom that she looks familiar to me.*

That wasn't it though. She might look familiar, but she really didn't look too much like Mom. Then it happened. Mom turned the page again. Bishop almost fell off the couch. It was the man. He was smiling and happy, and G-Ma Grace was sitting on one of his legs and laughing. But it was the same man. It was the man who told him to remember.

CHAPTER 2

ARE YOU KIDDING ME?

The smiling man was the man from his dream. Bishop leaned over and took the photo album from his mother and just stared. He began turning more pages, and the man appeared in lots more pictures. Everyone was smiling, hugging, eating, and laughing. It looked like everyone was having a great time.

Bishop turned to his mother and said, "Who is this?"

He was suddenly afraid to say that he knew this man and that this man was in his dreams.

"That," his mother said, "is your G-Pa Taylor. He and G-Ma died together in the car accident right after Thanksgiving. This was the last time the family was all together."

"Tell me about G-Pa. What was he like? I'm sure I don't really remember him. He looks happy in these pictures. Was he always happy?"

Bishop wasn't used to not telling his mom what was going on in his head. Normally, he would have told her what he was thinking, and they would have talked it out. Now he was afraid. Maybe he was crazy; maybe there was something wrong with him. How could he know this person who had been dead for so long—a person he hadn't seen since he was a very small boy?

Bishop's mom leaned back on the couch and smiled at him. It felt to Bishop as if she already knew what was happening in his head.

"Actually, Little, he was not always smiling. He worked very hard, and he would be gone for long stretches of time. When he was home, he tried to let go of his work, but sometimes it seemed to follow him. When it did, he was not laughing and happy. He was"—Bishop's mom seemed to struggle to find the right word—"driven. He worked so hard, and sometimes it seemed like he was angry with us. He wasn't. He was just working. He loved us all very much."

Bishop looked at the photo album for quite some time while his mom seemed content to sit and look too or watch him. After a while, Bishop handed the book back to his mom and went upstairs. He thought about the dreams he had, about the dream with G-Pa Taylor especially. Was it true? Did that dream really happen? He was thirteen years old! He was getting a little too old to have the thoughts he was having. He thought that he might be crazy or that there might be something wrong with his brain.

Sleep claimed Bishop as usual over the next few nights, but he didn't dream about G-Pa Taylor for almost a week. When he did, he tried to pay better attention. Instead of this being a dream that he had over and over, he tried to learn something new—and he did.

He looked at the big box and realized that the box wasn't big. It was smaller than a shoebox. It only felt big because he was so small. He also paid better attention when the box was opened. Inside the box, it wasn't fuzzy anymore. There were papers folded up. They looked really old and really worn. There was also a picture. It was G-Pa Taylor and G-Ma Grace when they were younger. He couldn't tell how old they were, but the picture was inside a glass paper-weight. The large bubble of glass made a dome above the picture of his G-Parents. He also got a better look at G-Pa, more details as it were. He was dark in the dreams before because of a large beard and mustache! When Bishop woke up, he wrote down all the details he could remember on the first piece of paper he could find—the back of his finished science homework.

"Mom, when you go to the store next time, I need you to pick me up a spiral notebook." Bishop was walking through the kitchen the next morning.

Bishop's mom looked at him like he was completely out of his mind. That made Bishop feel very uncomfortable until he realized what the problem was.

"Oh, never mind," he said as he headed for the grocery list.

His mom wouldn't remember, and she knew it. She had trained him to write down what he needed on the list. Verbal reminders didn't work so well. She never went to the store without the list though. If he needed it, he just needed to get it on the list. He decided to add something fun too, so under *notebook*, he added *cookies*. She smiled, then returned the milk to the refrigerator, and headed to the table to eat breakfast.

Bishop got his breakfast too, ate in silence, and got ready for school. At school, things were hectic: classes, athletics, frantically copying his dream to a sheet of notebook paper that he could take home, and erasing a strange and bizarre dream from the back of his homework—an overall busy day.

That afternoon when Bishop got home, his mom had apparently gone to the store because in his room, by his nightstand, was a blue spiral. It had his name printed on the front, just like all his school supplies did, in his mother's neat handwriting. Bishop wrote down the new stuff he had learned in his dream and had protected from Mrs. Covington, the science teacher—not that it was her fault that he wrote it on the back of his homework, but still.

Bishop was almost eager to go to bed that night and even got his shower in early, snacked quickly, and made sure a pen was handy. He wanted to remember everything he could about this dream—if he could just have it again tonight. He didn't, but two days later, he did! This time, he saw all the things that he had seen before, but it continued. This time, G-Pa Taylor showed him where he was hiding the box. In the floor, there was a part of the floorboards, near the wall, that had a very small hole. G-Pa Taylor used a piece of metal, stuck it into the hole, and pulled the floorboards up. He put the box inside the empty space. This time, Bishop knew it was a cigar box. He shut the floorboard slat and then patted the area with his hand.

G-Pa Taylor looked again at Bishop and said, "When the time comes, you're going to need to get this box. You know where it is, you know how to get to it, and you know that you need it. Remember! It's too important to forget!"

Bishop gasped awake. He fumbled for his pen and spiral notebook. He wrote down all the new stuff he had seen and heard. He leaned back into bed. It seemed that he was now keeping a dream journal. It sounded cool in his head but felt scary too. How many kids his age needed a dream journal?

Bishop's whole day was consumed with getting through the day, coming home, through the evening, and in bed again. He didn't even hang out with his friend after school. Jack was grounded for failing English class, and he was too eager to have a chance to dream again to hang out with any other friends. Over the next few nights, he was disappointed though. He talked to animals, flew, and walked around knowing what others knew; he even added a new dream. In this dream, he could control what others were thinking and doing. It was a cool dream, but it wasn't the dream he wanted to have. It was three more nights before he got what he wanted.

Bishop entered the dream right where he always did but now was impatient. He knew it was a dream. He knew what was going to happen. He was frustrated though. He wanted more details and didn't seem to be able to get them. The same talk from G-Pa, the same box, same hiding place—same everything. Something had to change.

Bishop asked his mom the next day, "Mom, I've got a strange question for you. I want you to take me someplace. That okay?"

Bishop's mom looked at him like, well, like he was asking her to commit to something before she knew what he wanted—which he was.

"Little, what are you up to?" she asked. "I think you better get the details of this request worked out a little better and bring it back for further review."

Bishop paused. He didn't even really know where the house was. "Mom, where did G-Pa and G-Ma Anastasi live? Was their house close to where we live?"

Bishop's mom almost dropped her glass. She turned and looked at him very strangely.

"Are you feeling all right? I know you've been having dreams. Are you upset by them? Are they making you sleep badly? What's going on?"

She was usually so laid back that you'd have to take her pulse to make sure she was alive. Right now, however, she looked strung tighter than a ten-pound weight on a string.

"I'm fine," Bishop said. "Really, I just have this feeling that I need to see that house in the picture. I wish I could explain it, but I really can't. It's just like I dream about the house, and I want to see how close my memory is. It's just one of those things. Maybe I don't really remember it."

Bishop wasn't exactly truthful. It wasn't the house that he dreamed about—just a small section of space under one of the house's floorboards. Just a box with papers and a paperweight picture.

CHAPTER 3

GETTING THE BOX

It was five days later, and Bishop couldn't believe his luck! He was in a car, with his mom, headed to Odessa, Texas. He didn't even remember hearing the name of the town. He only remembered hearing that they had moved when he was little. He didn't remember the move, just the information that it had happened. Mom had said she had business there anyway, and if he would behave himself, he could go.

Bishop wasn't sure why she was letting him tag along. He couldn't imagine what business she had to take care of. She worked from home on her computer, installing, updating, and maintaining security systems. She almost never traveled anywhere. Maybe she was going to troubleshoot for some company. Who cared? He was going where he wanted to.

The drive there was flat, brown, dusty, and full of weird-looking shrubs. His mom called them mesquite. He called them ugly. It just didn't look nice at all! He was used to at least a little bit of green and some type of break in the landscape. Not really hills, but just not total flatness. The Dallas-Fort Worth area boasted some pretty nice-looking areas, and where he lived in North Richland Hills was one of those.

It started with a five-hour drive, then checking into a hotel, unpacking, eating dinner, grabbing some snacks at the local Walmart, and settling in for the night. Bishop couldn't wait to get started; but his mother said she had other stuff to do the next morning and he'd have to watch movies, stay inside, and absolutely not open the door for anyone. A do-not-disturb sign hung on the door as she left. Bishop had not had any dreams, so he had not had to get out his dream journal. He didn't want to show it to his mom, so this was a perfect time to read over his entries. He just couldn't seem to learn anything new, remember anything new, or even understand what was going on.

Wow! Bishop was at his G-Parents' old home. Seriously? Cool! His mom said she phoned ahead to the people that lived in his G-Parents' old house and told them that she grew up there and was back in town. She just wanted to come see the old house, and did they mind? Apparently not because here they were.

Bishop rang the doorbell, and an older man answered the door. "Yes?" he said.

"Hello, Mr. Wilson. I'm Ellen Brown. I called you earlier this morning. I grew up here in this house."

Mr. Wilson looked at Bishop and Ellen. "Oh yes. I spoke to you, and my wife, Christin, spoke to you also. We were looking forward to you coming. Please, come in!"

They stepped into a house that didn't look anything like the pictures Bishop had seen when family was there. The dark paneling that had been in the house had been replaced by Sheetrock and textured and painted a soft green. While Bishop could tell it looked better than it had, it was also the first time he realized that he might have a problem.

Which room was it? He knew what it looked like in his dream, but did it look the same now? There was a window. He knew that. He also knew that he didn't know which window it was. He didn't remember looking out of it. Did it face the front, the side, the backyard, or the street? How was he supposed to figure out what room it was? What if there was carpet on it now? Bishop couldn't believe the complications he had never thought about.

Ellen Brown really wasn't paying any attention to Bishop; she seemed wholly focused on her old home. After a brief introduction of herself and Bishop, she stepped in front of Bishop and began talking.

It gave him a chance to compose himself and also to wonder again—
Why did Mom agree to bring me here?

The Wilsons introduced themselves, and Mrs. Wilson asked
them, "Would you like something to drink or eat? I've been making
cookies since I knew we'd have company. Would you like to look
through the house first? We've been doing some remodeling, so I'm
sure things are going to look a little different."

Bishop couldn't have been more frustrated—remodeling! Didn't
people ever just leave well enough alone?

"Let's look around first," his mom said.

She walked through the house, talking to the Wilsons about
what used to be here and what used to be there. The Wilsons loved
it, and his mom seemed to be having a good time too.

"Oh my goodness, here's where that heating grate used to be,
right here on the floor. It melted a pair of my shoes to it when I was
little. I was so cold, and the hot air blowing up from here was the
most amazing thing in the universe!"

Bishop looked at his mom. She really was into this whole tour-
the-house thing.

The Wilsons were telling her about updating the heating system
as Bishop looked around him. There was a door right by the front
door where they walked in, a door just to his left now along the
same wall, and a dining room in front of him with a kitchen beyond
that. None of it looked familiar. The dining room had a view to the
outdoors, but they headed down a hallway to the right and entered
another smaller hallway with bedrooms off it. Surely one of these
rooms would be the right one! Nothing looked familiar. Nothing.

Pale-beige walls, carpet along the floors—a total disappoint-
ment. Mr. Wilson kept up a constant stream of information.

"And then we changed all those old windows out with these
new ones. It was quite a job. Ha! It almost sounds like I did the work
myself, but I didn't," he said.

His wife began to laugh.

"No doubt!" she said. "After the fiasco in the front room, you're
just not allowed!"

Mr. Wilson turned a little red at this.

Mrs. Wilson continued, "He was sure he could do the remodel himself, so he began in a room we don't really use. The front room off the main living area when you came in. He just had issue after issue in that room. I finally told him that enough was enough and we were paying someone to do everything else. Since we don't use that room, we've saved it for last. We have people coming next week in fact. What did you use that room for, Ellen?"

Bishop's mom responded with a little laugh, "It wasn't really used for much of anything unless my father was home. It was his room, but there wasn't much in it. A chair, a folding table, and a file cabinet. That was it. He didn't even put rugs down."

"Can we see that room?" Bishop asked.

It just had to be the room he was looking for. Mr. Wilson looked a little annoyed, but Mrs. Wilson looked excited.

She must really want to make sure he doesn't start any more projects without her okay, Bishop thought.

"Now, Christin," Mr. Wilson started.

That's as far as he got though. Mrs. Wilson was already talking to Bishop's mom and walking toward the door closest to the dining room. When they walked through the door, Bishop's knees almost buckled. This was it. This was the room. This was where he had been told to remember. Now how was he going to get everyone else to leave and let him try to get under the floorboards? He had come prepared. He had a backpack and a variety of wire pieces. A bendable piece of silver wire from a model-car kit his friend had built, a piece of copper wire that he found in his dad's toolbox, and the ring from his three-ring notebook that had broken a few weeks ago. Surely one of these would open the secret compartment in the floor, right? His biggest problem would be getting everyone to leave him alone in there, right?

Wrong. His mother started asking questions about the apple trees in the backyard and the garden that had once been there. They all just walked out of the room, through the dining room, and out a door somewhere at the back of the house.

Bishop wasted no time. He walked right to where he knew the hole was for him to open the compartment. It was crazy how he knew exactly where to go. It was crazier how small the hole was! He had slung his backpack off and began unzipping it the instant the others had left. By the time he found the tiny hole, he had the pieces of wire and the binder ring out. The binder ring and the silver wire he brought was too big; he'd have to try the copper wire. The copper wire was thin enough to go in! He slid it in, bent the wire, slid more in, and pulled. The copper wire slid right out of the hole. This wasn't going to work! The wire was too thin! Bishop sat back on his legs. He looked at the tiny hole. It was taunting him! He was so close. He was just so close! Tears filled his eyes as the frustration took over. He could hear his mother's laugh from somewhere out back. He glanced in the direction of her laugh. On the floor, three feet away, was an old wire hanger. It was the kind that came with pants from the dry cleaner, but instead of cardboard along the bottom, it was just wire. It might work! It was sturdy, it was long enough, it wasn't going to be missed—it was perfect!

He grabbed the wire hanger and began to untwist the top. As soon as he finished, he realized he had another problem—the twisted section at the top would never fit through the hole in the floor. Luckily, Mr. Wilson had left tools in the room when he decided to stop remodeling. There were wire cutters, a hammer, a wrench, and a tape measure. Wire cutters to the rescue! In less than five seconds, Bishop had the cutters, cut the wire, and stuck it into the hole. He pushed it down about two inches, bent the wire, pushed it down another two inches, and pulled. The wire hanger started to unbend just a little, but the floor didn't budge. Bishop was afraid to pull harder. What if the wire hanger unbent all the way? He heard his mom's voice again—still outside but getting closer. He yanked the hanger, and dust went everywhere as the floorboard raised and dust from years gone by poofed out from it.

Bishop didn't think. He reached in, grabbed the box he knew was there, and shoved it, the hanger, the other wires, and the binder ring into his backpack.

He zipped it up as fast as possible and looked into the small space again. *Okay, good. Empty.*

He shut the floorboard and tapped it down to make sure it was even with the rest of the floor. Then he ran to the bathroom. He flushed the toilet as soon as he shut the door. Maybe they would think he had been in the bathroom all this time. Wait! They would think he had been in the bathroom this whole time! Gross.

He left the bathroom, flushed with more than just success— there was a little embarrassment there as well! The Wilsons fed Bishop and his mom some cookies and milk, and then they left to head back to the hotel. As they got into the car and drove away, they waved at the couple who stood on the front porch to see them off.

Bishop's mom asked, "Did you get what you were looking for?"

CHAPTER 4

INSIDE THE BOX

What? Surely she had no idea what he was looking for. Bishop was stunned. What could she know? She knew him better than anyone, but she sounded so sure of herself. He didn't know what to do.

"What do you mean, Mom? I don't understand." He didn't understand.

"Well," his mom answered, "you seemed to be looking for something with this trip. You know, like memories or closure or something." She calmly continued to drive them back to the hotel. "I just wanted to know if you found what you were looking for. Was the house familiar and all? You were so little last time you were there."

"Um, yeah, Mom. I guess I did find what I was looking for. The house was hardly familiar though. You know, all that remodeling they did and all. It just seemed to be any old house. That last room looked more familiar. Maybe it still looks a little the same."

His mom laughed. "I dare say it looks exactly the same as when it was Dad's office. He never really kept much in there, but it was his space. We kids steered clear of it, and he didn't usually invite us in. It's so funny that the room I remember the least is the only one that you remember at all."

Bishop didn't answer. He didn't know what to say. They arrived at the hotel, went in to pack their things, and left. His mom had only made the trip in person for him. She could have worked on the computer system remotely, at least that's what she had told him, but she chose to come down so he could make the trip too.

Bishop couldn't wait to get home! As anxious as he had been to get here, now he couldn't wait to leave. He had all his things packed. He had double-checked for stuff left behind; and he was waiting at the door, backpack in hand, for his mother to finish. Unusual isn't even close to how he was behaving—and yet his mother didn't tease him or ask what was going on. Bishop didn't realize until later how she simply got her things together as quickly as she could and got them on the road.

The trip home was long and boring. Bishop slept as much as he could, which wasn't much with his brain swirling around with thoughts and ideas on what kind of information would be in the box. He could hardly believe it had actually been there like in his dream. He wondered if the dream really happened or if he had come upon his G-Pa at some point when he was putting it back into the hiding place and he just conjured up the rest of it.

Finally home, Bishop took his things inside, unpacked all his stuff, and waited to be alone with his box. Mom made it easy—again. She and Dad went out to dinner! He was alone with his box. He went to his room and turned on the light. He dug his backpack out of the back of the closet. He had put it there as if he were all done unpacking earlier. He pulled everything out—the wires, hanger, and binder ring, mixed up with some papers and the glass paperweight that must have fallen out of the box on the trip.

Things had shifted around in the box. He had been as careful as he could be with the backpack, but the box hadn't been securely closed. So some stuff was in the box, and some was dumped out at the bottom of the backpack. Tossing aside the wires and hanger and binder ring, Bishop concentrated on the contents of the box. He opened the box and took out the remaining papers. The box smelled funny. Old and was lined with red velvet lining. It had not a musty smell but something else. Bishop realized it had been a cigar box, so the smell must be old cigars.

He looked at the glass paperweight first, half fearing and half hoping he would see a picture of his G-Pa Taylor and G-Ma Ruth.

He did. It was the same picture in his dream. He had thought the picture in his dream was a little fuzzy and distorted but quickly realized his dream was clear. The picture was fuzzy and distorted because it was old, grainy, and the glass oval that sealed the picture inside made the picture distort slightly. It was like looking in the mirror at a funny house. He piled all the letters together in a stack and looked at them. Some of them looked very old. Some of the letters did not look nearly as old as the others. He was almost afraid to start reading. He began to turn the letters over, looking at the front and back. He didn't know how to sort them or where to start. He was glad he was sitting down when he turned one of them over and saw his name written on the outside of the letter. He sat looking at it for several minutes before he finally opened the letter.

Bishop,

> If you have this letter, you have the box. This means you and your whole family may be in danger. You are special, and you are different from others your age. If you want to find out more about yourself and your family, you can. Just read the letters. Learn as much as you are able about the Talent in the family and what Talents you may have. Some letters will be difficult. Do not falter! It is important that you do this, learn about your past, and do the right thing in the future. This is in your hands now. I love you so much,

> G-Pa Lincoln

It seemed to Bishop that the weirdest part of the letter should be that his dead G-Pa had given him a memory as a young child and knew he'd find this box. However, the word *Talent* kept swirling through his mind.

Bishop sat there for a while. He was looking around but not really seeing his room. The blue walls, the blue curtain that his mother had made, the *Star Wars* poster that featured Yoda telling everyone the things they really needed to know in life they learned from *Star Wars*. Baseball trophies from when he was younger, some hockey bobbleheads, and a piggy bank that oinked when you put money in. Instead, what he was seeing was the letter. Over and over in his mind, he was seeing what the letter said. He hardly had to refer back to the actual written words. *You're special. You're different.*

Was this letter even from his G-Pa? He had not been raised in the age of innocence. He knew there were weirdos out there. He knew they could concoct elaborate schemes to get what they wanted. Isn't that why Mom got the big bucks for designing security systems? Bishop was confused.

What was this about? He wasn't special. He wasn't more athletic than others; he wasn't smarter than others. He wasn't even the best at his instrument in band! How could he be special? Also, how could he not sit and read the other letters one right after the other?

CHAPTER 5

READING THE LETTERS

Bishop knew Mom and Dad would be out to dinner for about another hour or so. There was plenty of time to really look through these letters. If some were difficult to read, that would be okay; he'd have plenty of time, right?

Bishop could not have been more wrong. As he folded the letter from his grandfather up and put it back inside the envelope, he began looking at the other letters. He spread them out on the bed, carefully, and decided he could only begin picking them to read at random. So eeny, meeny, miney, mo!

The next letter Bishop picked up was at one time sealed with wax and a signet ring. The wax was long gone, but the brownish stain and slickness was left behind. The paper itself was very strange. It was much thicker than he was used to; and it had a rough texture to it which was, Bishop assumed, another indication of the letter's age. It was written with very poor grammar and in a sort of difficult-to-read cursive. Bishop though it might be called calligraphy. So this is what his grandfather meant by "difficult."

to mine own offspring,

i has't hath found mine own talent. i am a communicat'r. if 't be true thee has't talent, thee shall findeth t at which hour thee cometh of age.

26

rememb'r to bid thy offspring and carryeth on
the traditions. if 't be true thee has't nay talent,
gaze thy offspring. those gents may has't what
thee doth not. keepeth t closeth. keepeth t secret.

Henry
1508

Bishop read through the letter haltingly at first and then was
able to read more easily after several readings. Some words made
some sense, and other words made sense because of context only.
Bishop thought about English class, context clues, and all that his
English teachers bored into his head. Although he loved reading, he
preferred to choose his own books—English teachers rarely let that
happen. He did, however, feel a wealth of gratitude at this moment.
He managed a basic translation.

To my offspring,

I have found my Talent. I am a
Communicator. If you have Talent, you will find
it when you come of age. Remember to tell your
offspring and carry on the traditions. If you have
no Talent, watch your offspring. They may have
what you do not. Keep it close. Keep it secret.

Henry
1508

Bishop looked at the clock. It had been half an hour. Maybe
there was time for another letter? Surely he could do another one
before his mom and dad got home. He picked up the next letter. It
too was difficult to read, but it was instantly recognizable as written
by a girl. Bishop wasn't sure why he knew that, but it just looked like
a girl's writing. He scanned to the bottom. Sure enough, it was signed
by a girl named Elizabeth Howard. The scrolling writing was just as

difficult as the one before, so he set it aside. Surely there was one he could actually read, right?

The next letter was even worse! It was signed John de Gaunt. Bishop had no reason to keep at letters that were so hard to read, so he kept looking.

Success! Here was a letter that was much easier to read. Bishop settled in to read. It wasn't long, but it was longer than Henry's.

Salem Village
March 12, 1692

Dearest Mother,

To this death, I must go. Pray care for the child. Lest she should then be a victim of this. I am at fault, for I told a girl what was coming her way. For this, I burn. Hast thou not told me to not speak? Hast thou not told me I would be judged? The man her father was giving her in marriage to wouldst have killed her. How do I silent stay? How do I allow the death of a child? No more than thirteen is she! For this, I burn. Tell the child of my life. Do not linger on the death, 'tis done. Talents I have may pass to the child. Knower and Finder am I. Protect the child. Pray teach silence. May the child heed silence better than I.

Your loving daughter,
Bridget Bishop

There were many more letters. Bishop was overwhelmed. He was reading the last words of someone who was being burned! He knew enough history to know this had to be tied to the Salem witch trials. So someone with Talent was mistaken for a witch and burned. He didn't have the heart to read anymore.

Bishop knew these needed to be put away. Where should he put them? He didn't really think hiding them well was a problem; he just wanted them put away so his mom wouldn't see them at first glance. The backpack still seemed like a good idea; so back in the box they went, the box into the backpack, and the backpack into the closet. He tossed his summer reading book on the top. That should make it clear there was nothing interesting in there—if his mom even looked that far in.

CHAPTER 6

INFORMATION OVERLOAD
OR UNDERLOAD?

His parents came home, and as he had to decide what to tell them, he decided to tell them nothing. There was nothing he could see they would do other than ask questions he couldn't answer. Maybe his mom knew something, but he had a sneaking suspicion this was about him, not his mom.

Why was this happening? All this information, Talents, long-dead people—it just wasn't making sense. Bishop felt overwhelmed with it all. He wasn't even a small part of the way into the letters he had, so what else would he learn? He played some video games and finally went to bed.

That night, the dreams were the same—and new. He flew; but it wasn't like a bird with all the flapping of wings, arms, or whatever. It was more like it came from his gut and propelled him up. He used his arms a little like swimming to get started. The air was more solid for some reason, but most of this power to fly just came from inside.

New to the dream was a darkness. The darkness had people in it, and they were calling to him. Not for help but to come and talk, take a break from flying, and just stay awhile. He couldn't see them but could hear and feel their presence.

When he woke up, that part of his dream shook him a bit. It was strange and different, even for him. He wrote it in his dream journal and got ready for his last day of school. Tossing his journal in his bag, he headed out the door.

Bishop was glad to almost be done with school but not glad to be cleaning. I mean, who knew they were going to have to clean? Not him! Athletic lockers are the grossest of the gross, and his was not above average in cleanliness. In fact, it was so cluttered with old junk, mismatched socks, socks that actually did match but he didn't want to bother taking home, pens, pencils, and old homework assignments he had gotten back graded, as well as old homework assignments he had forgotten to turn in that he simply emptied the whole lot into the trash.

Looking down into his hands, he realized the cleats were so far gone they weren't worth salvaging. He had literally run the outside edge off each shoe. He must run really crooked, he thought as he saw them hit the bottom of the trash can.

"Let's go, guys. There are only twenty-five minutes left in this block, and you guys are not done!" hollered Mr. Molina, the substitute they had for athletics the last few days.

Coach Long had been out with a new baby the last couple of weeks. Mr. Molina was finishing off the year, and he'd been fun. Not really a coach, so the guys got to do what they wanted during athletics, which was usually to sit and watch the cheer girls as they worked with the next year's cheerleaders.

"Let's go! Each of these lockers has to be washed down, and the top lockers can't be washed until the bottom lockers are empty! You'll not be released to the gym until you finish!"

Well, the girls were in the gym; so every male, including Bishop, hurried up. He even started dragging stuff out of Jack's locker; it was two over and one down from his.

"Dude, how do you have so much stuff in this locker?" Bishop asked.

Jack just laughed. "Oh, look, that assignment I thought I turned in. The one that made me fail English for the three weeks!" Jack said as Bishop smacked him in the back of the head.

"Idiot!" said Bishop. "You could have passed and not been grounded!"

31

Bishop was not feeling forgiving at this point.

Jack just shrugged. "Only a couple of more days of this. I've done the math on it. I'll pass."

Just like Jack. He did what he had to do to pass. No more and no less. This progress report fail was unusual. But it was a progress report, so Jack didn't really care. Bishop's mom would have lost her mind, so he didn't mess around as much as Jack.

All the guys around were finally done, and they were using the rags and bucket of soapy water to give the lockers a very quick wipe down—again, the minimum. After we finished, we all tossed our rags into the buckets and headed out to the gym to watch the girls.

CHAPTER 7

DODGING THE BULLET

W aiting for Jack to get ungrounded was a drag. First day without school, and he had to resort to hanging out at the park with no one in particular. It was hot and boring, and there was no good reason to stay. There was nothing to do at home either unless you counted cleaning, and Bishop didn't. Report cards couldn't come soon enough. He headed back to the house.

Bishop stood transfixed. He wasn't able to walk or run or breathe. All he was able to do was stare at the vehicles that were in front of his house—the vehicles that screamed disaster like a tornado siren. He began to walk on shaky legs; he began to run. He was a full block away. A very, very long block away. All he could think of was the burning desire to be at his house. He was running, he was running, and he was suddenly there. He had been halfway up the block; now he was here. Instantly.

As shocked as he was, he gathered himself to enter the house. It was scarier than anything he had ever done in his whole life. What would he find? Who had been hurt?

Bishop whipped open the front door and charged into the house. He was unable to form words; his fear had clogged his throat. The paramedics were just pulling the stretcher from on the ground to its upright position. Somebody was on it. Bishop began moving to the side; there was a man's voice coming from the kitchen. It sounded like the man was talking to his—yes, it was his dad. Then, that meant his mom…

He moved to the side of the exiting paramedics and closed into the stretcher. He was horrified at what he might see. He was looking at the floor. As he looked up, he saw blood on the sheet of the stretcher, then a very hairy arm, and the face of his substitute teacher, Mr. Molina. Bishop jumped back from the stretcher and tore around the corner of the living room and into the kitchen. There was the policeman and his father, sitting at the kitchen table. He looked to the side; and there, making coffee like people were attacked in her house every day, was his mom.

"Mom!" Bishop yelled as he completed his turn into the kitchen. "What happened?"

Bishop's dad stood and followed Bishop to his mother. As Bishop embraced her, his dad embraced them both.

"It's okay, Bishop. Don't worry. We're all fine." Mom was calm as could be.

"What happened?" Bishop was still shocked. What had happened in his house?

Ellen moved out of the embrace and glanced back at in the direction of the door. Even though she couldn't see the door for the kitchen wall, Bishop could see that was her target for the glare.

"Some full-blown idiot broke into the house. I guess he thought we were gone and had just forgotten to—oh, I don't know—close the garage and take the car with us?"

Sarcasm. It could get thick at this house, but Bishop appreciated the attitude. It helped calm him down that Mom just seemed really irritated. Then he remembered the blood.

"Dad, what did you do? Did you shoot him?" Bishop asked. He knew they had a couple of guns, but they weren't exactly out for everyday use.

The police officer spoke up at this point. "You have got that part wrong, son. Your dad didn't have anything to do with this at all, well, except for calling the ambulance. He did do that." The policeman chortled for a second. "Never seen anything quite like it. What type of training have you had, Mrs. Brown?"

It seemed the police officer had gotten his dad's story and was moving on to Mom.

Mom actually laughed. "I didn't have any training. I had older brothers, a couple of them. I might have been protected from every other male on the planet, but those two made sure that although no one else could touch me, I was their own personal punching bag. I learned to fight back really quick. I got fast, smart, and strong. Haven't lost it apparently."

Bishop's dad put his arm back around her and said, "Never figured you did. Why do you think I don't worry too much when you go out in the evenings to walk?"

Bishop knew his mom had nerves of steel. He knew she could wrestle him to the ground in a heartbeat. He also knew that if someone had threatened him, she would have absolutely lost her mind.

"Mom, so why did Mr. Molina break in? What was he doing?"

Now it was chaos. No chaos when the paramedics were here. No chaos when the police were taking interviews. No chaos when Bishop got home. Now there was chaos because he knew the person that had broken in.

The policeman began asking questions left and right. Bishop was trying to answer. But the questions were coming so fast, and his brain felt foggy. Too much had happened too quickly.

Bishop's mother finally said to the officer, "Hand on a second. Let him sit, have a soda, and start at the beginning and tell you everything he knows. Then you can ask him questions."

Bishop told everything he knew, which really wasn't much. Mr. Molina had been his substitute in athletics class for few days. He had been nice and talked to the guys while they were cleaning. He had not spent more time with Bishop than any other students, and he could not remember seeing Mr. Molina outside school anytime before today.

"So he's not been one of your regular subs?" the officer asked, looking over the notes he had taken.

The ambulance had long since left, and Bishop was feeling tired.

"I mean, I don't pay attention to subs in the building unless I have them as a teacher. He could have been in other classes, but this was the first time I have had him."

Bishop's answer seems to mollify the officer. Another officer came in the front door.

"Anderson, we found a car a couple of blocks away. I don't know if he planned to rob the place of only light things he could carry or if he was scoping the place out for a later date. It looks like a rental, and all we found in the car was a water bottle, a GPS unit with this house's address, and this spiral notebook."

As the officer held out the spiral, Bishop started.

"That's mine!" he blurted out.

It was too. It had his name printed across the front of it in his mother's neat handwriting. It was his dream journal. He hadn't thought about it in awhile because he hadn't been having any new dreams lately. Still flying an awful lot and talking to some animals, but nothing so disturbing as the dreams about the box had been.

"I must have thrown that spiral out when I threw out my old school supplies in the locker room at the end of the last day of school. Why would Mr. Molina pull it out?"

"Do you think this Mr. Molina may have come over this way to return the journal?" one of the officers, Bishop thought the other guy had called him Anderson, said. "I can't imagine that he would drive this way, park so far away, and then not bring what he was going to return with him. What did he say to you when you discovered him, Mrs. Brown?"

Ellen looked at the officer. "He was coming down the stairs, and he saw me, grinned at me, and then charged. I don't know why he grinned, but he wasn't grinning when he left! He attacked me, and I fought back."

"What's in this notebook of yours?" the other officer asked. "Is there something top secret?" The officer grinned at Bishop. "Does it at least have your address and explain how the guy decided to come here?"

Bishop paused; the officer began flipping through the spiral. Bishop bit back the urge to tell him to give it back or to grab it from him.

Instead he simply lied. "It's just some ideas for a book. I like to read, so I thought I'd write down some ideas, you know? Nothing major. Just some cool flying stuff."

Ellen turned her head toward the pantry, away from where the officers were standing. Bishop wasn't sure, but he would swear that she was laughing.

She turned back. "Yep, our boy can tell a tall one. He was the biggest liar this side of the Mississippi River when he was little. We got him that spiral because we figured we should put that imagination to work."

The officer simply handed the spiral back to Bishop.

He grinned. "Well, don't want to mess with a budding author. Here's your spiral, and Mr. and Mrs. Brown, here's your copy of the report we have filled out. We will be in touch for more information if we need to. There was no sign of forced entry, only one person, and no property stolen. When Mr. Molina wakes up, he will have to make a statement to tell his side of what happened. Then a decision will be made about taking him into custody. Pretty sure that decision will be that he should be taken into custody."

Bishop's mother had begun to sputter and was on the verge of interrupting when the officer was talking about making a decision whether or not to take Mr. Molina into custody. Bishop was pretty sure he knew what Mom was thinking. It would have been something like, "I will not be held responsible for what happens to that man if he comes back here." Mom just didn't play—as evidenced by the drops of blood on the floor in the front foyer.

CHAPTER 8

Having "The Talk" with Mom

Since there were very few things in the house to eat and it was way past time for lunch, Bishop's dad decided they should all go eat together, go grocery shopping together, and then come home together. Bishop had a sinking feeling that the rest of the summer would consist of way too much together time.

He was halfway through his nachos when he remembered all that had gone on this morning before Mr. Molina had come: the letters, Talent, and the weird sensation of being in one place and then suddenly being in another. He didn't know what his dad knew, but he knew his mom knew a lot. She also knew he was full of questions for her.

After lunch, Mom helped him out by getting them out of grocery shopping. "Greg, I'm tired. I'd really rather go home than go shop. The list is done. Do you mind?"

Bishop's dad didn't mind at all. After he assured himself that she was just tired, not hurt, and the grocery list was indeed complete and that she would lock all the doors and not leave the garage open, he agreed. He even agreed to leave Bishop at home instead of having him come to help him with the groceries.

When they had gotten inside the house, locked the door behind them, and given Dad a thumbs up, Bishop's Mom turned to him and said, "Okay, Little, there's a whole bunch that happened today, and we need to talk about it. Do you want anything before we have a seat? We're likely to be there awhile."

Bishop wasn't interested in a drink or anything other than a conversation with his mom. Most of the time, conversations with Mom were okay and somewhat fun sometimes, but he didn't look forward to them quite like this.

Ellen sat on the couch, and Bishop sat on the opposite couch facing her. She looked at him for a few minutes.

"I'm not sure where to begin actually. I guess I need to tell you a little bit about your G-Pa Anastasi."

"I need to tell you something before you take your turn," said Bishop. "When we were at the old house, I found a letter addressed to me from G-Pa."

His mother's eyes got big, and she looked at him for just a second. "Oh. Well. Now, that's good, right? Okay." She was shocked and surprised. Very rarely did that happen. Then she laughed. "Dang it, Dad," she said as if he were in the room with her. "You always did say my brain was slick as an onion."

Bishop looked at her. "Mom, you've said that for years. 'Slick as an onion,' and I don't get it. You'd think that with all that has gone on, I'd be more worried about letters from the past and someone breaking into the house, but I'm really not. What does 'slick as an onion' mean?"

"Well now," she began, "your grandfather used to ask us if our brains were slick as onions when we did something that was, well, less than intelligent. Okay, downright dumb. Anyway, the theory was that each time you learned something, you'd put a new wrinkle in your brain. If your brain is 'slick as an onion,' you haven't learned too much."

Bishop laughed and said, "Of all the things I've learned today, that has got to be the funniest. 'Slick as an onion.' Wow."

"Okay, Little, what have you learned today?" his mother asked. "You've gotten a letter from your grandfather. Seen this debacle with Mr. Molina. What do you know, and what do I need to fill in for you."

"Well, Mom, I learned that we are supposedly descendants from a long line of 'Talents.' These Talents have different abilities, and sometimes not every person in the family has them. I mean, that's really all I know. I mean, he only left me a letter. Oh! I also know he thinks our family could be in danger because I know this?"

Bishop did not quite feel like showing her the entire box. He didn't want her to know about the box at all. The box seemed somehow like it really needed to stay a secret.

"Some people only have one Talent, and some people have multiple Talents. These are called Omnis. You may be an Omni. We need to begin to teach you to block."

Bishop's eyes got wide. "Is that what you did to Mr. Molina? You blocked him?"

"Hmm," she replied. "I didn't block Mr. Molina. He attacked me, and I hit him. Then I added insult to injury by kicking him a couple of times."

Bishop winced. He knew that Mom could be tough as nails, but the image of her doing that just made him cringe. This was his mother—he should be helping to protect her!

Bishop's mother dismissed his thoughts. "Little, I'm fine. You're fine. And there's a lot to cover. Let's just get down to the business of Talent. That's what we need to talk about. Before we discuss anything else about your G-Pa, let's talk about blocking.

"You are becoming powerful. You will start to project that power from your mind. Someone who is sensitive to that power will be able to track you with it. The more you mature, the more powerful you will become. Let's talk about how you'll block.

"When you are first learning, it will feel silly or weird or something in between. Trust me, you will get better at it and feel it working soon."

Bishop looked at his mom; he was determined to do well. He just still didn't know what to do. She was looking at him in silence. Were they supposed to be blocking?

"Um, I'm not blocking right now, am I? Am I supposed to be?" Bishop asked. He was worried he wouldn't do well.

"No, I was just thinking," his mother said. "You've had a lot going on today. Blocking will make you tired when you first learn it. I was wondering if today is really the best day to start this."

Bishop began to panic; she had to teach him! Before he could get his half-formed protests to leave his brain through his mouth, his mother continued.

"It's just too important to put off anymore. Anyway, here we go. Little, close your eyes."

Bishop obeyed. He felt stupid, but he obeyed.

His mom continued, "You have to *feel* your brain. It can't just be a body part. It has to be an entity in itself. Feel your pulse in your brain. Feel your heartbeat in your chest. Follow it along your veins. Keep with the pulse. Follow it into your brain. Can you feel your pulse yet?"

Bishop felt very stupid. "Um, no. I know I have a heartbeat, but I don't know how to 'find' it."

To his relief, she didn't laugh. "Bishop, put your hand over your heart. Find your heartbeat." She paused, giving him the chance to follow directions and begin to "feel" his heartbeat. "Now," she continued, "feel it. Get used to the way your heart is beating. Feel the rhythm of your heart. Just sit and feel it for a minute."

Bishop's eyes were closed, his left hand over his heart as if he were saying the Pledge of Allegiance. He was still. All he felt was his heartbeat. It was strong; it was rhythmic. He felt the pattern of his own heartbeat.

"Now, Bishop," his mother continued, her voice low and soft, "follow your heartbeat. Feel the beat leave your chest. Follow the blood through your veins and into your head. Feel the beat move along your veins. Follow this. Follow the beat."

She closed her eyes as if she were finding her own heartbeat, but Bishop didn't see this. He was engrossed in feeling the beat of his heart and following it along his veins.

"I have my heartbeat!" Bishop exclaimed.

He never opened his eyes, but his mother did. She saw the look of fierce triumph. He was getting the hang of this.

"Good!" she replied. "Follow it."

Bishop was following his heartbeat. It moved along his body in a slow and steady pace. *Dum-dump. Dum-dump. Dum-dump.* It was climbing through is body. It was in his brain. He could feel his heartbeat in his brain!

"I've got it, Mom. I can feel my heartbeat in my brain."

"Excellent, Bishop. Now feel the blood pumping all through the brain. Concentrate on the blood pumping along the outside portion of your brain. Just between your brain and your skull. Feel that. Feel that area of your brain. Feel the blood all around your brain. Feel your brain encased by your blood."

Bishop did. He could feel the blood coursing through is body, but he could now isolate the blood and feel the part he wanted to while ignoring the rest. He felt the blood around his brain and only around his brain.

"Soon, you will not need to concentrate so long to find your heartbeat. Soon, you will be able to feel the blood around your brain with almost no effort at all. You will not have to concentrate so hard, and you will not have to consciously think about it all the time. This is blocking. The barrier in you that will keep others from finding your or invading your mind is in your blood. If you surround your brain with your blood and maintain that feel, you will be able to block almost all the time."

Bishop sat on the couch across from his mother for a long time. He felt for his heartbeat and followed it to his brain time and time again. He would let go, or the ability to focus would be interrupted sometimes. He just started over. It was very relaxing. It could almost make him forget all the other questions he had for his mother.

CHAPTER 9

A MOVER

Of course Bishop didn't put his questions off for long. He practiced blocking for the next little while with his mom and then while he was unloading groceries with his mom and dad. It really was much more difficult to block when doing other tasks at the same time. However, it led to another realization for Bishop. His next shocker came while putting up the Oreo cookies.

"Bishop," his dad said, "hand me the gallon of milk."

His dad gestured toward the cabinet with the milk on it. With one leg holding the fridge open, his dad couldn't reach it. Bishop could though.

"Got it dad," Bishop said as he grabbed the jug and turned around to hand it to his dad.

At that point, he's lost his concentration and stumbled. He quickly righted himself and passed the milk jug to his dad. Bishop grimaced. How long would it take to get good at this and stop losing his balance when he tried to do more than one thing?

"Son, you're going to get better at blocking. Don't worry." Bishop's dad, who was always there for him but never said much, had just spoken to him about blocking! "This scar on the side of my head? Well, I got that one when I was learning to practice blocking and happened to also be riding my bike. I took a tumble from the bike and got up close and personal with the brick mailbox at my house. Your G-Ma Brown swore if I kept trying to learn to block while I was moving around so much, she'd beat me with a stick till all the leaves fell off. It takes time. Just stay off bikes while you're learning it!"

His dad grinned at him and closed the fridge. The last of the groceries were put away, and his dad was leaving the kitchen.

"Um, thanks, dad!" Bishop said. "I'll be sure to stay off of—well, I don't have a bike, but I promise not to steal the car and try to drive!"

His dad laughed and kept going as his mother was reentering the kitchen. Bishop was surprised by his father's advice, not because he didn't think his dad knew anything about blocking but because having never talked about it with his dad, only his mom, he just didn't expect it. It was nice to have one more person to know what was going on. One more person to talk to about things, you know, if kids actually talked to their parents. He chuckled quietly. He was *that* kid. The one that actually held conversations with his parents—on purpose! He should have known he was different.

"So you're not planning on stealing the car, huh? That's good news, one less thing to worry about." His mom was grinning, but her words still disturbed Bishop.

"I know there's a lot to worry about, Mom, but I have some more questions for you."

Bishop was ready to get more answers. It really was nice to have someone else to talk to, but it felt like his main contact in all of this right now was his mom.

His mom snagged a cold soda from the fridge.

"Want one?" she asked.

Bishop did want a soda—and a whole lot of answers. They sat down again, but this time, at the old oak kitchen table. It was scarred, dented, and showed signs of what his mother called "love" and his father called "abuse."

"So today when I saw the police cars and the ambulance, something funny happened. I was so freaked out and so worried that something had happened that I had a hard time getting started to run. But when I did, I was running as fast as I could, and then when I was still half a block away, I suddenly appeared here. I think I may have transported. Problem is, I don't know how I did that or how to control it. What if I just start transporting all over the place?"

Bishop's mother gave him the gift of not laughing at him.

"Son," she said, "It's not really that easy to Move. I'm not saying you didn't Move. I'm just saying that it's not likely to just happen. You won't just Move because you think about being somewhere. You had adrenaline in your system in what I would guess was a pretty large amount. That gave you the ability to Move even though you don't have the control or ability to do it anytime you want. You'll learn to control it, but it may be awhile."

Bishop thought for a minute, slowly turning the can of his drink on the scarred tabletop. "So I'm going to learn to control it, but I can't now. Also, the only reason I did it earlier was because I had so much adrenaline in my body. So what else am I going to start doing? How long before I have control of my Talent?"

"Control is one of the hardest things to learn. Are you blocking right now?" Bishop's mother asked.

"No," Bishop answered. "I forgot."

"Okay," his mom said, "pick up your heartbeat and begin to block again. You're learning to control blocking. It's the simplest but one of the most effective defenses we have. It also takes control. Learning to control your blocking will help you as you learn to control the other Talent that you will have. Bishop, you will have other Talent. We may not know which ones, but my mother said there would be more and that you would be strong. You're presenting at about the age we would expect, and you could continue to discover Talent until you're around twenty-five. That gives you ten to twelve more years."

Bishop couldn't help but laugh. "So what you're saying is I'm discovering my seriously abnormal Talent at a normal time. Glad to know something is normal!"

Ellen smiled, almost a sad smile. "Bishop, it will feel like your world has changed in an instant. It hasn't really, but there are some things that have changed. Never think you are alone though. I may not have Talent, nor your father. But we know others who do. We know what you're going through. It won't be easy, but it doesn't have to take over your life either. You are still you. Just with a few additions."

"Mom, I think I'm starting to understand all this. It's just a lot and really quick. Why didn't you tell me about this before? Why did you wait so long? I could have totally been used to this and been blocking since I was little. This wouldn't have been so new if I had known all along. If I had known, maybe I would be less overwhelmed and more in touch with my Talent already."

The more Bishop said, the more aggravated he got. This should have been easier. They should have prepared him for this!

"Now hang on there, Slick," his mother said. "This was not a decision I made on my own, nor did your father make this! This decision was made when you were very little, and most of the family was involved. I may not always understand the different Talents that others have, but I have learned to trust my family and Greg's family. And we've done the best we could. I know you're upset, but this was not kept from you to punish you in some way.

"Little ones are the most vulnerable to problems. Since you're supposed to be so strong, the family felt that you should be kept ignorant as long as possible. When your hormones kicked in and things started to disturb you and you began to have power surges, these were the things we were looking for. We knew it was about to happen. I got you to Odessa as quickly as possible. You think I didn't know what was happening? Think again. I may not have known exactly what you needed to do, but I knew you needed to go. You don't even have to tell me all that happened. Dad just told me years ago you would need to go, and I should take you to the house. You can get mad, but it's not going to change what happened. It's not going to help you handle this better, and it's not going to make you look very mature either. So choose. Nasty attitude or work on blocking?"

Bishop was mad. He was very mad. There were some things kids should be told. Things like they're a freak of nature. However, he wasn't blocking. Again.

"I am mad, Mom. I don't even really know where to aim it." Bishop looked at his mom for a moment, picked up the thread of his heartbeat, and began to block. "I'm going upstairs. I need to think and practice blocking. I also want to write some of this stuff down. If I write it and then read it later, maybe it will make better sense."

His mom got up from the kitchen table and retrieved his dream journal from the coffee table in the living room.

"Here, son, use this for now. It may be time to look into getting something a little easier for you. Maybe a laptop? It's going to need a great system on it if you're going to be using it for this, so that will take some time. Now, move your rear end upstairs."

"Um, Mom?" Bishop looked at his mom like she had surely lost her mind. "I don't know how to Move yet, remember?"

Bishop's mom laughed. "That wasn't the type of move I was thinking about. I was thinking about when you use the huge feet your father gave you and take the rest of your body up the stairs."

As Bishop walked upstairs, he realized his mother had not been calling him "Little" all afternoon but "Bishop." Did she finally feel like he was growing up? Maybe he was no longer her little boy, just her son. Somehow, the difference in what she called him felt deliberate, like she was acknowledging he was growing up. He has always felt like he was more grown-up than his parents gave him credit for, and her using his name all day made him feel like maybe she was seeing it too.

CHAPTER 10

A GREAT ESCAPE

The telephone ringing woke Bishop up. He didn't get up to answer it. They almost never answered the house phone. Anyone that knew them always called the cell phones, and since that only left telemarketers, nobody would rush to answer the phone. They only kept the house phone so that they could run one of the security systems for the house off it. Today was a little bit different though; the phone only rang two times before somebody answered it.

It wasn't very long after that Bishop's mother came flying up the stairs to his room.

"Bishop! Are you in there? Are you all right?" She sounded like she was about to panic. Rather than waiting the two seconds it would take him to answer her, she simply burst through the door. "Oh, why didn't you answer me?" she said.

"Mom, you have to give me enough time to take and breathe and then push it over my vocal cords!" Bishop answered. "What's up? What's wrong?"

"Well," his mother said, in a much calmer voice, "it seems that the police will not be arresting Mr. Molina for breaking into our house."

"What!" Bishop exclaimed. "Why not? It was clear that he broke in or at least entered without us wanting him here."

"It seems," she answered as she sat down on the foot of his blue-and-red quilted bedspread, "that the police are actually unable to arrest him. Not that they are unwilling." At the blank look on Bishop's face, his mother continued, "He has left the hospital. He's not in his room. They can't find him anywhere, and they've been unable to locate him on the security camera posted in the ambulance bay and the front and emergency entrances. There are other exits, so it's quite possible he just left. However, he left without any of his things."

"So he left in a hospital gown?" Bishop asked. "Um, he's gonna be flashing underbritches to people!"

Bishop knew exactly how those hospital gowns worked. They flapped open in the back and let everybody know what kind of underwear you were wearing. When he was seven, he broke his arm and was admitted to the hospital while they tried to determine if he needed surgery, to have it set, or to just let it mend. Lucky for him, it just had to be casted and mend on its own. Unlucky for him, he had to walk from the room he was in down the hall to the bathroom, and everyone saw his Power Rangers underwear. It was embarrassing. After that, all the character underwear went away, and solid colors replaced them. You never really knew when you'd be at the hospital. It was just best to be prepared with solid-colored underwear.

"Bishop," his mother said, "I think the bigger problem than him flashing his drawers is that he is not in custody. We don't know if he's planning on coming back here or not. Your dad has decided to stay home from work today, and I'm not scheduled to be out of town for several days. So we're going to be very vigilant for the next few days."

"Dad got the guns out?" Bishop asked.

"Yes, actually," his mother answered. "He does have them out. We are not leaving them lying around though. We really don't expect Mr. Molina to come back here, but you never know. He may have had help escaping, so someone else may head over. It's also possible he has done whatever he came to do, and it's all over for now. We just don't know. I would like you to follow directions really well though. If we yell at you to do something, could you just do it?" Bishop's mom smiled at him. It was like she wasn't even talking about the possibility that a man could be coming to their house to do them injury. "Bishop, keep blocking, okay?"

Bishop simply answered, "Okay."

Over breakfast the next day, Bishop's dad was continuing a conversation that must have begun quite early in the day. He launched right in without filling Bishop in at all as to what they were talking about.

"Fine," Greg said. "If that's what you want, do it. But I'm not taking care of any of that stuff. I don't like them, I don't want them, and I won't be doing anything for it."

Bishop's mom answered, "No problem. I think we've got it covered. There will be ground rules, but I think it's a great idea and will help with the state of things here."

Bishop looked from his father to his mother and back again. They were apparently done and satisfied with their decision; he just didn't know what they were talking about.

"Hey," Bishop's mother said to him, "you blocking?"

He wasn't. He looked at her for a second trying to decide whether to just say yes and start blocking or whether to own up that he wasn't doing it right then and start.

His mom laughed. "Too slow. You're not blocking. Start now." She got up from the table to get the juice.

As they continued to eat, his mom told him about the next part of their day. "We're going to run a few errands today. I want you to come with me. Not because I think you need to be with me because of Mr. Molina, but I think you should have a say in this decision."

"Okay," Bishop said.

It felt like that might be all he really had to say today. He finished up his breakfast and pushed the book he was reading to the middle of the table. It was a great adventure book, but right now, his life was enough of an adventure. He wasn't sure he wanted to read about anybody else's!

He went upstairs after breakfast, brushed his hair and his teeth, felt too lazy to wash his face, and got dressed in mostly clean clothes. He wasn't sure where they were going, but he was pretty sure he wouldn't spend too much time out of his parent's sight. He was right.

"Bishop! Get yourself down here!" His mother's voice called from somewhere in the general direction of downstairs.

"Okay!" he answered.

He wondered for a minute if he should try to see how far into his day he could get only using that one word. Then he decided it might be the only fun he had today. He better give it a try.

CHAPTER 11

WARM, WET, COLD

While Bishop's mom drove, the game continued. His mom would make a statement or ask a question and Bishop was able to answer with just "okay."

His mother said, "I want to stop for a drink. You want one?" Bishop's answer? "Okay." His mother ordered his favorite drink without any input from him. So far, so good.

His mother said, "Let's have tacos for dinner tonight." Bishop's answer? "Okay."

His mother said, "I've got to stop for gas. You want to pump it?" Bishop's answer? "Okay."

His mother said, "You need to keep practicing blocking too." Bishop's response? Yep, it was "Okay."

Bishop was almost to the point of laughter. How long could he keep this up without her noticing and without cracking up? He wasn't sure, but between practicing blocking and making sure he didn't laugh, he was unable to pay enough attention to where they were going.

His mother said, "Okay, Bishop, we're here. Get out and come in with me."

Of course Bishop said, "Okay." He snickered just a little as he said it and thought he might get busted by it. He didn't though. His mom seemed pretty preoccupied at the moment. He followed her into the large metal building through the front double glass doors.

He was concentrating very hard. Block, block, block, don't laugh, don't laugh, don't laugh. It just wasn't an easy thing to do!

His mother spoke to the lady in the front at a small desk. It was more cluttered than his room, and that was saying something!

He flopped down in one of the chairs that lined one wall and grabbed a magazine off the table. The first one was about cats. He tossed that back. He wasn't too interested in cats. The next one was about horses; it too went back to the table.

As Bishop reached for the next magazine, his mother said, "Come on, Bishop."

And he lost his composure for a moment. Luckily, his mother's back was to him when he said, "Okay."

He followed his mother and the lady down a short and very white hallway. He heard some creaking and squeaking noises. It took him a second to put all the sounds and the information his brain had been ignoring together. They were at the animal shelter!

This revelation was made as they walked through another glass door into a room full of cages. The cages were floor to ceiling and about four feet by six feet. There were a couple of dogs to each cage. He finally started paying attention to his mother and the lady they were with.

"Okay, so you want a medium-sized dog, and if it was a protective-type dog, that would be good, right?" the lady from the front was talking to his mother.

Bishop walked around the cages. He was fascinated by the dogs. There were only about eight dogs total in the room. There were several small dogs, but Bishop knew they weren't considering that. He had paid enough attention as the lady talked to know at least that much. He went over to the cage that held the two larger dogs. One was at the door, jumping and yapping at him. It looked like it was part-German shepherd, part-something else. It had the coloring of a German shepherd but not the size. The other was about halfway back into the cage, along the side of the cage that didn't have dogs next to it. The dog was looking up at him although its head was down. It was a deep chocolate brown, with curly hair.

"That is the one." Bishop knew instantly which dog should come home with him. He pointed to the dog whose head was hung low but whose huge, warm brown eyes were following his every move.

"Well, this one here is a more lively dog and will be a great playmate for you. She'll want to run and play and will love you like crazy." The lady pointed to the dog at the door, the one that was still yapping and jumping.

Bishop's mother looked at him.

She looked at the two dogs and turned to him and said, "Well, if you can say something other than 'okay' today, you can have the dog you want. We'll take the brown one."

Bishop looked at his mom and laughed. He should have known she paid enough attention to realize he was answering everything with "okay." He was so excited! He was getting a dog! So this was what his parents were talking about at breakfast. His mom must have been arguing that the house would stay safer if there was a dog.

The lady looked at Ellen. She looked at Bishop, and she looked back at the dogs.

"Listen, folks, I know you want the brown one, but this one here would be a better guard dog than the other one. Brownie came to us from the ASPCA, and she was abused pretty badly. She's a good dog and sweet as can be, but she's probably not ever going to be a good guard dog."

Bishop didn't care what the lady said. He just *knew* that this was the one. What if his mom didn't listen to him? He couldn't explain it, but he already felt an affinity with this dog. This was the one. Before today, he never knew this dog existed. Now, he wasn't sure what would happen if he didn't get to have this dog. He looked at his mother—she was looking at him.

"Bishop, pick your dog," she said.

She knew he realized. She knew that he felt something, and she was going to let him pick. There was no second-guessing the decision. There just wasn't. The brown dog was coming home with them.

They walked back up to the front with the lady to fill out the appropriate paperwork. Bishop felt bereft already; just being away from the dog was painful right now.

"Okay, while Keisha gets your dog, you fill this paperwork out. There's the adoption fee and the starter kit fee. You're going to leave with the dog, a small bag of food, a choker leash, and a small food and water dish. You'll probably want to get some nicer stuff for her soon. Some people get a dog and realize it's a mistake the first few days. If that's the case, they haven't spent too much money and can bring them back."

Bishop's mother listened closely as she filled out paperwork. Bishop paced back and forth in front of the door they had walked through to see the dogs. He was wondering what was taking so long.

His mother had just finished the paperwork when a doctor walked out with the dog.

"Hi, I'm Keisha. I'm the vet here. Here's your dog. She is in pretty good shape, but when she came to us she had a severe ear infection. Actually, both ears were infected. She's doing better, but she will need to finish taking these pills and continue her ear cleanings. One pill twice a day for the next four days. She will need her ears cleaned daily for that same time and another ten days after that. She is not in pain anymore, but I'd like you to bring her in for a follow-up visit in the two weeks or so. It will be free of charge and is part of your adoption. All the directions to complete treatment are written down and in the adoption paperwork. Other than that, she's in great shape physically. Warm body and a cold, wet nose."

Keisha handed his mother the pills, a large while bottle, and a bag of balls and handed him the leash.

He got down on his knees and looked at the dog. She didn't approach him, and he didn't approach her. They just sat and looked. Bishop looked at her whole body but not into her eyes. He wasn't sure why, but that seemed wrong. They simply studied each other.

The lady that had taken them to look at the dogs turned to Keisha and said, "Have you seen anything like this? I swear I figured that dog would just pee the floor and run for cover. Here she is sitting all pretty and just looking at this boy." The lady turned to Ellen and said, "Your boy must be good with dogs. This one has been so skittish I really didn't think you'd get out of here with her, but there she sits, just looking at him like he's a dog treat."

Finally, the dog stood up and began to move. She didn't sit on Bishop; but she walked over, turned slightly, and sat beside him. She looked at everyone else around them and laid down.

"Well," said the doctor, "don't that just beat all."

They had finished the paperwork, gotten their dog and her things, and headed out the door.

After they had loaded in the car, Bishop's mother looked at Bishop and said "How about we hit Petco now and get her some real food and water dishes, a cute harness, and a good leash?"

Bishop simply couldn't resist. "Okay."

They both laughed. They walked through the store and picked out a red harness. As they continued through, they passed a row of toys. Having no idea what the dog might actually like, they sat on the floor trying a couple of different toys. She wasn't impressed with the chewy bone, nor did she get excited about the KONG cone thing that had a hole for peanut butter. All that changed when Bishop squeezed a multicolored octopus. The dog's head came up, ears went up, and her whole body responded to the sound. Clearly, they had found a winner. In addition to the harness, they now had a squeaky ball and the squeaky octopus and were looking at leashes. Again, Bishop went straight to red. His mom teased him a little about getting pink, but Bishop was firm—nothing pink! New food dishes and a large bag of dog food along with training treats completed their purchase.

CHAPTER 12

CONFRONTATION AT THE PARK

Bishop woke up the next morning after having another strange dream. He had been with his new dog, and they had been at another house. There was an old man there with them. Bishop couldn't see him well, but the old man was hitting a puppy. The puppy was the same color as his new dog and cried piteously. Bishop had tried to stop the old man, but he couldn't touch him. He would get close, and there was a barrier between them. He was frustrated and yelling at the man to stop, but the old man just kept yelling and hitting the little puppy.

Bishop was grateful to wake up from that dream. It was disturbing to him, and he couldn't shake it. He didn't write it in his dream journal because he didn't see the point. It was only one dream. If it repeated itself, he would write it down.

Bishop's day was about to get better. He went downstairs with the dog and let her outside. He grabbed some cereal and his book from the counter and had a seat.

His mom walked into the kitchen, opened the door for the dog, and said, "Well, rumor has it that report cards were mailed day before yesterday. That means that they should come in sometime today. Jack should be ungrounded then, and I'm sure you'll be spending lots of time together now. We need to talk about this."

"First things first," his mother said with a serious face. "What are you naming this dog. I refuse to continue to call her dog."

Bishop started laughing. Of all the things he thought might come first, it wasn't what he expected. Fair enough though, this beautiful dog needed a name.

"Girl? Brownie like they called her at the pound? Maude?"

Bishop could tell his mother was kidding, but the names were so ridiculous to him he felt very protective of his new girl. He leaned down, looked at her, and tried a couple out.

"Katniss? Annabeth? Bella?" Nothing seemed to impress his new friend, so he tried again. "Jane? Elsa? Elizabeth?" He was running low on options for sure. He couldn't think of another literary option for a girl dog off the top of his head. "Sophie?"

Something magical happened, the dog looked up, at him, and began to slowly wag her tail.

"Hey, Sophie. Hey, girl!" he said.

She got up, got as close as she could to his leg without actually being his leg, and leaned in.

"Okay, Mom, problem number one is solved. Her name is Sophia. Sophie for short. Now what?"

His mom stopped him in his tracks with just one word, "Jack."

"What? I promise not to tell Jack anything. I know it'd just be dangerous, and he probably shouldn't know anything."

Bishop's mom smiled. "Well, I'd rather you didn't say anything just yet. You've been apart for almost four weeks now. He failed at progress report, and now with final grades coming out, you've not spent more than five minutes together lately. We just need to talk about how you're going to handle this.

"Remember that you're still to keep blocking, and you need to keep practicing that. You might even tell Jack that you've been having some headaches and this is an exercise the doctor has given you to help. Think up something smart though. Jack's no dummy, even if he did fail English at the progress report!"

Bishop laughed, "Yeah, he's no dummy. He's just a dummy! It's been a bit of a bummer without him. I haven't gotten to tell him about what happened with Mr. Molina or anything!"

Bishop's mom smiled. "Actually I told Joan about it already, so I'm sure Jack knows. You are going to have to be careful around Jack.

You don't need to tell him much about what's going on. Number one, he won't believe it, and he'll think you're crazy. Number two, he may say something to someone else not realizing what a problem that could cause for you. It might make it hard for you guys to pick up with the same easy friendship you've always had. It could cause a strain. Just be aware. Talk to me if you have any problems or questions about what to say to Jack."

"Okay, Mom," Bishop said, "I will. Also, even though you haven't asked, I am blocking right now. Just so you know."

His mother laughed as she got up and left the room. Bishop's breakfast was done, and he was eager to watch the mail for report cards. He couldn't wait to get to just hang out with Jack.

Sophie followed him through the house and back up the stairs to his room. He had no intention of changing out of his cotton pants, but he figured he should get something out just in case Jack came over. He grabbed a shirt and a pair of jeans and tossed them over the end of his bed. He pulled up the blankets on his bed without truly "making" it.

Bishop brushed his teeth, actually washed his face this time, and began to pick up his room before he realized what he was doing. Kids don't just pick up their rooms. They make messes, but they don't clean—unless they've been threatened by their parents. That's when Bishop knew he had to get outside. If he stayed in, no telling what horrors he might face. It started with cleaning his room; could it spread to cleaning the bathroom? Better not take the chance!

Five minutes later, dressed and bored silly, Bishop stood on the front steps staring at the mailbox. "Soph, the mail doesn't come until around one o'clock. There's not much point in watching for it! Let's go for a walk!"

Bishop was glad to see Sophie was at least as ready to do something as he was. He grabbed her leash and hooked it onto Sophie's harness. He was so glad he had bought red leash and harness and not let his mother get crazy and go for the pink-studded one. He would have looked ridiculous!

Down the block and toward the park was really the only place to go. Sophie was so excited to be out she'd run ahead of him, then start sniffing a tree or bush, and end up way behind him. It was a constant cycle of sniffing, running, sniffing, running. Bishop couldn't remember feeling this content in the last few days. He was blocking. He was walking his dog—a dog he'd wanted for so long—and he was pretty sure he'd see Jack later today.

As he walked into the park, Bishop noticed that there was someone at the table under the awning. For a moment, Bishop was really irked. He hadn't realized until then that he'd been planning on heading to the tables and sitting down for awhile. He wanted to think about what was going on and make plans about what to tell Jack. These things seemed pretty important to Bishop right then. The person sitting at the table turned to look in Bishop's direction, and every other thought flew out of his brain. Mr. Molina was back.

He was bruised up and looked like he was hurting pretty bad. He didn't get up but turned his body to face Bishop.

"I don't know how much you know, Bishop, but I'm not here to hurt you", he said. "I have studied you for a while, hoping that you didn't develop the powers that can be so dangerous in the wrong hands. Your grandfather is a mastermind and will be using your powers to hurt others. You don't know him. You can't trust him. I will give you information that will clear up at least some of your questions. I have it here in this envelope." Mr. Molina pulled a large manila envelope off the table beside him and moved it closer to Bishop. "I hope that you will spend some time studying this and understand that you're on the wrong side. You're innocent. You can't be expected to know, but you've got to see before it's too late. I was sent here to give you this information—you need to read it."

Bishop was stunned; he didn't really know what to say or do. His first instinct had been to run, his next to yell, and his next to read the information in the Manila envelope. Sophie had plans of her own though.

As Bishop stood dumbly looking at Mr. Molina, Sophie growled low in her throat. Her front legs bowed up and out, her chest expanded, and her hind legs went down. The bark started a nanosecond before the charge. Sophie was out for Mr. Molina's blood, just as surely as his mother had been.

Bishop held onto the leash but just barely; as Sophie charged the short distance through the green grass to the cement slab that held the table, Mr. Molina jumped up and winced. He began to back away as Bishop walked forward slowly and let Sophie get closer. The park was deserted except for the three of them, so Sophie's bark and charge were not bringing the attention they would have if the park had been crowded. Bishop was still unsure what to do.

"Just read the information." Mr. Molina said. "It will change how you feel about everything."

He turned to go, and limping slightly, he made his way to a car a short distance away.

Bishop squatted down on the grass, putting his weight on the heels of his feet, held onto the leash, and began talking to Sophie. "You're amazing, Sophie! What a good girl! What a good dog you are! Come here, Sophie. Come here, girl. That's a good girl."

Sophie had ignored him at first but stopped barking and sat down watching Mr. Molina until he got into his car. Once he was in the car, Sophie turned, wagging her tail, and walked over to Bishop. She walked right up so close she gave him a good bump. The bump was enough to send him spilling backward into the dust—into a pair of legs he never saw coming.

"Dang, dude, your mom bought you a killer!" Jack said.

CHAPTER 13

JACK'S BACK

Bishop just stared up at Jack for a few seconds trying to grasp what was going on. First Mr. Molina was at the park giving him yet more information. Second, Sophie was a full-blown killer. Last, but not least, Jack was on the loose. Weird, sweet, and sweeter.

Bishop struggled to his feet, grasping Jack's hand for a lift up. Sophie stood back up at the same time. She was not in full "attack mode" anymore. In fact, she seemed a little frightened of Jack! She stood and walked behind Bishop—keeping him between herself and Jack. Her head was hanging low, and she wasn't looking at either Bishop or Jack.

"Dude! Your dog just totally attacked Mr. Molina! That was awesome! Did you see Mr. Molina's face? Did your mom do that? What did he want? Do you want to call the cops?" Jack's sentences just kept pouring from his mouth like some primeval waterfall—nothing could stop it. "What's your dog's name? Does she always attack? Why doesn't she want to kill me? Let's go tell your mom!"

Bishop finally stopped the flow of words with a simple statement—"Jack, shut up." Bishop started laughing. "Okay, let's take my killer dog home, tell my mom what happened, and see what she says."

Bishop had almost forgotten the Manila envelope by this point. Seeing Sophie turn into a raving maniac and seeing Jack was almost enough of a shock to forget that he had just been talking to Mr.

Molina and had been given yet another piece of information. He was crazy glad to see Jack but needed to focus for a moment too. He stepped up, grabbed the envelope, and turned back around. Jack had a quizzical look as Bishop began to walk back toward him.

"What's that?" Jack asked. "What's in there, and why was it so important that Mr. Molina would risk coming within fifty miles of your mom? And the cops too," Jack added on.

"I don't really know what it is," answered Bishop truthfully.

He really didn't know, and he wasn't planning on finding out with Jack around. His mom was right. This wasn't going to be easy. How do you have a friend and keep such a huge secret without tossing the friendship out the window? Bishop wasn't sure he knew. He figured that was just one more thing to add to his I-have-no-idea list.

Jack just kept standing there. "Dude! Open it! Then we'll know what it is!"

In a not too distant past, Bishop would have done just that, but now he hesitated. How did he avoid opening it in front of Jack, and did he really want to show his mom? Mr. Molina said he was on the wrong side. Was Mr. Molina right? Jack was presenting a huge problem in the first two minutes they were together. If Jack wasn't there, Bishop would have time to think. But that wasn't the case, and Bishop had to come up with something quick.

"Jack, let's go back to my house. I want to put this up. It may have evidence or something they can track Mr. Molina with." *Okay,* Bishop thought, *that was sounding a little flimsy.* "Or," Bishop said, "I might not want to tell Mom about it. You know she's going to get freaked out. Do we really want to get her all riled up again? She's a bit on edge right now."

The second argument seemed to carry a lot more weight with Jack than the first one had. There were not too many people that would intentionally set off Ellen Brown.

"Yeah dude, let's go to your house and look at it and then decide if we want to tell your mom or not."

Jack was nothing if not practical. Look and then decide. What could go wrong, right? Um, everything? Who knew what was in there or what it would tell Jack. Bishop knew the walk home was going to be a frantic scramble to think of a way to not tell Mom, not let Jack see the envelope, and not let either know that something was being kept from them. Wow, life sure was simpler a few days ago.

The boys headed home with Sophie hot on their heels. She was not running ahead and sniffing, nor was she getting far behind. She was just walking a foot or so behind Bishop, who was walking on the sidewalk. Jack, who was walking in the street beside Bishop, kept looking back at Sophie as they talked.

"So," Bishop said, "finally ungrounded, huh? It's about time. This you-being-grounded business is not my idea of a good time. Next time you think about not doing your work and failing a class, think again! Your mom might actually bury you under a large rock if you failed for a six weeks! If this is what happens when you fail for a three-week progress report, an actual failure on your report card might send her over the edge."

Jack laughed. "Yeah, my mom can join your mom on the edge. Do you know how cool your mom is right now? I can't believe she broke Mr. Molina's nose! Mom told me about that. Crazy."

Jack laughed again and shook his head, continuing to take sneak peeks at Sophie.

CHAPTER 14

LIAR, LIAR, PANTS ON FIRE

Although they walked quickly, it seemed to Bishop that the walk took forever. But by the time they got home, he had a plan. When they came through the garage to go into the house, Bishop put his finger to his lips while looking at Jack and stashed the envelope behind the large cabinet that his dad had stacked with tools. Nobody would find it there in the next little bit, and he didn't want it in his hands when he walked through the door.

As Jack and Bishop enter, Bishop's mom is in the kitchen making cookies. Bishop knew she stress-bakes, but is that what's going on?

Bishop said, "Hey, Mom! Look who Sophie and I found today?"

Jack pops in with "Mr. Molina!"

Ellen dropped the cookie sheet a few inches onto the stove top, spun around with wide eyes, and yelled, "What?"

This was not the way Bishop would have broken the news to her, but Jack was not as careful. The chaos broke out as Ellen began to call her husband, shoo Jack and Bishop to the kitchen table, and hurry to shut the garage door which Bishop and Jack had just come in.

She yelled at Greg to come home and immediately dialed the police.

While she was telling them what happened, Bishop said to Jack, "Way to go, knothead. Now we are going to be stuck inside all summer. What were you thinking?"

Jack hung his head a bit but also had a smirk on his face. "Aw, come on, man! You know they'll calm down, and it was fun!" Jack was unrepentant.

Ellen began to ask questions but stopped. "Just wait a second, and the police will be here. They had a unit just down the street," she said.

The doorbell rang not fifteen seconds later, and Ellen rushed to answer the door. The officer who arrived was not one of the two who had come before but someone new. For some reason, Jack was uncomfortable when he arrived. He immediately remembered he was supposed to be blocking and got right on it. The officer took a glass of water from Ellen, had a seat with the boys, and pulled out a notepad and recording device.

"Okay, boys," said Officer Johnston. "Let's start from the top. Please tell me everything you can remember starting from when you boys left the house."

Jack, of course, interjected immediately. This time, Bishop didn't mind. He didn't want to talk to this officer for some reason.

Jack said, "Bishop left first and walked his dog to the park."

The officer looked at Bishop and asked, "Is that correct?" to which Bishop simply nodded yes and continued to block.

Jack picked back up the story. "When I saw Bishop, I was several houses from the park. I saw the dog trying to attack someone, and Bishop walking closer to let the dog scare him away. I caught up just in time to see it was Mr. Molina."

Officer Johnston turned again to Bishop to verify.

This time, Bishop responded verbally, "Yes, that's correct."

Officer Johnston held his gaze and said, "Tell me more."

The intensity of his stare right into Bishop's eyes made him very uncomfortable. It felt like he was watching it all happen again and hearing it too.

Bishop finally broke the gaze and looked at his mom. "Mom, could I have a Dr Pepper? I'm thirsty."

His mom simply handed he and Jack drinks and told him to keep going.

Bishop knew, somehow, there was something wrong; this guy was—he couldn't put his finger on it—wrong. He looked at his Dr Pepper and began to talk.

"It is exactly the way Jack said," he responded. "I walked to the park, saw Mr. Molina, and Sophie started barking and lunging. I let her get closer because Mr. Molina was clearly afraid of her. After a few seconds, Jack came up behind me, and Mr. Molina had left."

"Did Mr. Molina say anything or give you anything?"

Bishop was worried Jack would say something, so he began to answer very quickly. "No. He just asked me what I was doing. Sophie scared him, and he left. I don't know what or if he wanted anything from me."

At this point, Ellen asked, "Are other units looking for Mr. Molina?"

Officer Johnston leaned back and much to everyone's surprise said, "No, we wanted to be sure it was a credible sighting before we dispatched units."

Bishop, Jack, and Ellen all looked at him, horrified and at a loss for words.

He continued, "It seems to be, so I will radio for backup and search the area."

Bishop thought his mother would explode, but she simply said, "Please do and hurry. I'd like to see him apprehended."

While Bishop and Jack stared at each other, Ellen silently walked Officer Johnston to the door and returned.

"Jack, call your mom to come on over. I was making cookies for when you boys were done," said Ellen.

CHAPTER 15

MANILA ENVELOPE

After Jack and Joan were gone, Ellen turned to Bishop. "Okay, we both know there was a problem with Officer Johnston. I need to know what's going on."

Bishop, still unsure what to say about the envelope, simply told her about his feelings about Officer Johnson, "I don't know, Mom, there was something off about him. He made me uncomfortable. When he looked at me, it was like he was rewatching the incident through my eyes. It felt like he could see and hear everything. I had been working on blocking, but it was still happening. I mean, I think it was happening. That's when I asked for a drink to get away from him, and that's why I didn't look at him again."

His mother seemed to pause and consider what he said. "There is clearly something going on, but I just struggle to think the police would be anything except impartial on this. Mr. Molina should be in jail, and his delay may mean they miss him altogether."

At this point, his dad got home, and Bishop got up to go upstairs—with a slight detour to the garage to get the envelope.

He settled on the bed with Sophie curled up beside him. Her presence made him feel better as he opened the envelope. He wasn't sure what to expect, but this certainly wasn't it. Inside the envelope was another envelop! It was bubble wrapped and also sealed all over with packing tape. Weird. It only took a couple of minutes to get through all the tape—carefully. When it was opened, more letters spilled out. Bishop couldn't believe it. They were mostly very, very old, and some were written in a different language altogether. No way would he be able to decipher these as easily as the others.

One envelope, however, was modern and easy to read. This one was the letter from Mr. Molina, and it was addressed to him.

Bishop,

> *Please look at these letters and decide for your-self if you are on the right side or not. Your family has a history of harming mine. This goes back not decades but centuries. It is time to stop the harm, stop the madness, and only you can do this. Read "The Prophecy of the One." We believe it is you. Do what you were called to do. I will support you in any way I can. I will look for you again soon.*

> *—Molina*

Bishop really couldn't believe what he was reading. His mind was absolutely spinning and couldn't seem to land on anything for very long. His family hurt Molina's family, and what was he talking about when he said he thought Bishop was "The One"? A fight between the families, and it went back for centuries? The One? His mind kept landing on that particular part.

He went down for dinner, answered a few questions from his dad, and took Sophie for a walk. It was only a few houses down, across the street and back. No way were they letting him go far. He was *hoping* to run into Mr. Molina. He had questions he wasn't even sure how to ask. He really wanted to just listen to what was going on because he felt totally overwhelmed. His walk was, unfortunately, uneventful. As he curled up on the bed with Sophie later that night, he was looking for answers in his dreams. No answers were to be had, but he did dream about the mean man and the poor puppy again. Yelps, cries, whimpers, and screams were not what made for a restful night.

CHAPTER 16

Now Errrbody Knows

The next morning, for whatever reason, he had no interest in reading the letters. He had enough to think about. It was summer. Jack was able to come over, and he just couldn't bring himself to read them.

As Bishop went downstairs to let Sophie out, he heard his mother getting off the phone. His mother's conversations weren't usually interesting, so he didn't even wonder what was going on. She talked to her friends all the time and about the most random things. Chicken salad recipe? Sure, that'd be a conversation she'd have. Which store was having a sale on yarn? Oh, she'd be in on that conversation. When/where her girlfriends were meeting up for choir practice, even though he'd never heard her sing at a choir concert? Again, he just didn't care!

He and Sophie went outside for a few minutes and, then, headed in for breakfast. For some reason, Sophie liked to eat while they were eating. It was really funny to him.

"Bishop," his mom said, "I've got an update for you. Well, more of some information. Are you blocking?"

Bishop hung his head a little. Of course he wasn't blocking. He took a second to find his heartbeat. He felt it strong; he followed the beat to his brain and felt the blood course around his brain and protect him.

"Yes, I'm blocking," he answered and then added a very quiet "now" to that.

His mother simply smirked. She was no dummy, a fact he had to remember as he was navigating what to tell her and what not to.

"So," his mother continued, "Joan is also Talented."

Of all the things she could have said, this would not have been what Bishop was expecting to hear.

"What? Joan? What about Jack? Is Jack Talented? How do you know?" Bishop was flabbergasted at this turn of events.

"I have known Joan was Talented since she moved here. In fact, she moved here because she is Talented." Ellen settled into her chair, with her bowl of cereal, and began eating.

"Mom! Quit playing. You're just going to sit there and eat cereal and not tell me anything else?"

Bishop was so immediately frustrated at his mother. It sent a flash of adrenaline through his system. His mother's eyes widened when her spoon whooshed out of her hand and hit the floor.

"Keep blocking. You are transmitting really loud right now." Ellen's eyes were still wide as she watched Bishop.

He felt out of control, and powerful, and mad, and his head really hurt.

He gasped. "Gahhh!"

His mother came around the table and grabbed his shoulders. "What is it? What's going on?"

He just looked at her for a second. He was no longer mad but a little scared.

"It's my head. It just started hurting really bad, and it startled me. It still hurts."

"Breathe. In, out, in, out. Find your heartbeat. Slow it down. Concentrate. Slower, slower, slower, breathe, slower. Breathe slower. Block."

She stepped back and allowed Bishop to regain control. He did. And although he remained surprised and uncertain, his head wasn't hurting, and his heart rate had slowed.

"Mom, what just happened?"

His mother sat back down, grinned at him, and pushed her mostly soggy cereal away from in front of her.

"That, my boy, was your Talent brought on by adrenaline and frustration. You will have to learn how to control it, but that was a very strong first Move."

Bishop replied, "I moved the other day, remember? This isn't my first move."

His mother smiled and responded, "Yes. You moved yourself, but this time you moved another object. Most Movers only do one or the other."

"Well, are you going to tell me about Joan or not? I want to know what she does."

His mother didn't respond immediately but was looking at him.

Finally, she said, "What would you guess she can do? I mean, looking back, is there something that she was always able to do that stymied you and Jack?"

Bishop thought but didn't remember anything unusual. Jack's mom seemed perfectly normal.

"No, I don't really remember anything she did that seemed extraordinary. I mean, we never go away with lying about going someplace and going somewhere else, but that's something all moms do, like the 'eyes in the back of the head' thing."

Ellen began to laugh. "You nailed it. She's a Finder. She always knew where to find you boys, and that's how you didn't get away with stuff."

So much of his childhood made sense. They were so careful in their plans and always busted. Freaking Finder.

Bishop chuckled and then gasped. "JACK! Is Jack Talented? What is his Talent? Why did you say we couldn't talk about it? This doesn't make sense!"

Ellen nodded her head sagely. "Yes, it doesn't seem to, but it really does. Joan has said Jack has potential, but he has not blossomed with a Talent. I didn't let you tell him because I really needed to speak with Joan first, and now we both agree that Jack should be told. She is telling him this morning, and I'm sure he'll head over when she's done."

Life was immediately better for Bishop. There is nothing like the feeling of a best friend, and having to worry about what to tell him was starting to stress him out. This would be way better. Bishop wondered what Talent Jack might have and mindlessly began eating his super soggy cereal. He was coming up with all kinds of cool thing his friend might be able to do and realized he didn't really know the range of Talents very well.

Learning more about Talents seemed really important all of a sudden.

"Mom," began Bishop, "what are the possible Talents? I mean, what could Jack possibly do?"

Ellen smiled. "There is quite a range, actually. I have a paper that goes over it fairly well. When Jack comes over, why don't the two of you check that out? It's an older paper, but it's fairly comprehensive. I'm sure it would be good for both of you to check it out."

Bishop began nodding his head, wondering if this "older" paper was as old as some of the letters he had upstairs.

CHAPTER 17

ALIEN NATION

It wasn't too long after Bishop had brushed his teeth and kind of made his bed that the front door was rattling and then the doorbell was ringing. With all the events of late, Bishop was startled and began heading for the stairs.

Greg yelled, "Don't!" as he headed for the door.

Greg was to the side of the door about to peek out the corner when Jack's voice was heard.

"Why is the door locked? Lemme in!"

Greg smiled and began to open the door as Bishop headed down the stairs. Jack burst through the door but stopped when he saw Bishop's dad.

"Oh, hey, Mr. Brown. Sorry about that. I thought you'd be Bishop."

"Yes," Greg responded as he shut the door behind Jack, "clearly," as he rolled his eyes, chuckled, and said, "Go on, boys. I'm sure you have stuff to talk about."

Boy, did they ever have stuff to talk about. Bishop was expecting Jack to be angry that he didn't tell him first and he had to hear it from his mom instead of his best friend, but Jack couldn't have cared less. He was too busy being excited about possibly being Talented and wanted to know more about Bishop's Talent.

"So Mom told me you're a Mover. You 'moved' down the block when you saw an ambulance at your house. Is that it? Do you have any other Talents?"

Bishop grinned. "At least I get to be the first to tell you something!" He then related the story from earlier that morning with the spoon and explained that moving yourself was different from moving objects.

Jack listened with rapt attention and then asked, "So can you just move stuff now? Like, move that pillow over here. I could use it."

Bishop laughed. "No, it doesn't work like that. I don't have any real control yet. It only happened because I was frustrated, angry, and had a lot of adrenaline in my system. I can't do it at will!"

Jack thought about that for a moment, then grabbed a dirty sock off the bedroom floor, and threw it at Bishop's head while he was sitting in the chair and said in a deep voice, "Send me the pillow!"

For a brief second, Bishop thought Jack was serious, then realized he was trying not to laugh, and began laughing himself. Sophie was startled by the sudden noise and jumped in Bishop's lap immediately. Once they started, they couldn't stop. Jack, lying on the floor in Bishop's room with his feet propped on the bed, and Bishop in the lounge chair to the side were laughing hysterically when Ellen knocked on the door. They just couldn't seem to stop or get up to open the door. After a couple of seconds, Ellen pushed the door open. She was holding some papers in her hand.

"Okay, chuckleheads," she said, "here are the papers. Give them back when you're done."

She smiled as she walked the few steps to the chair and handed them to Bishop. By this time, the boys were howling about her calling them chuckleheads. Everything just seemed hysterical. As they stopped laughing and Bishop soothed Sophie, he realized that the relief at having his best friend back and being able to share all this was the main reason for all the laughter. He threw the sock back at Jack and explained what the papers were. They both agreed they needed food (it had been almost an hour since breakfast at this point) and it would be easier to look at the pages at the table, so they headed downstairs.

At the table—with a huge bowl of buttered popcorn, two blue-berry muffins each, a Dr Pepper each, and a jerky treat for Sophie—the boys began to read.

Talents:

Knower—Gets thoughts or impressions when speaking to people. Can often tell the truth from a lie and is often labeled a "psychic."

Finder—Able to find people and/or items when they are lost. Sometimes an item of a person is required when finding people. Often labeled a "psychic."

Mover—Able to move self and/or objects. Effort required to move the original object is often a limitation on what can be moved.

Traveler—Able to bend time and move from one place to another. Limits: cannot occupy the same space in time as another version of you. Information on travelers is rare. Travelers must also be Sourcers—it is believed they must source the energy for their travel before they go.

Sourcers—Able to harness energy from living things around them to use. In and of itself not a usable Talent. Must be combined with something else to be useful. Energy can be stored in certain stones.

Changers—Able to change the way they look or sound. People unable to control this were often thought to have multiple personalities.

Speaker—Able to speak with / communicate with
other living beings.
Omni—A combination of three or more Talents.
Rare and often labeled as "insane."

The boys looked at each other and then began the discussion.

"So you are supposed to be an Omni then, right?" Jack asked.

Bishop nodded affirmative and responded, "I am a Mover. That much I know. Does moving self and moving objects each count as a Talent? I mean, that would be two of my three."

Jack shook his head no as he spoke, "I mean, it says 'and/or.' I guess you're the 'and,' and it should only count as one."

Jack continued to study the list, reading and rereading each one in turn. "Okay, so Mom is a Finder, clearly. Do you think that's what I'll be? I mean, is that how it happens? Parents pass along their Talent to their kids?"

Bishop had no clue, so he called in reinforcements.

CHAPTER 18

LESSONS IN GENETICS

"Dad! Where are you?" Bishop called as he walked from the kitchen to the living room toward his parents' room with his new faithful shadow Sophie following right behind.

"Upstairs" was the faint reply he received.

His parents' room had a private study in it that was above their bedroom.

Sounded like dad was there, so Bishop walked to the bottom of those stairs and hollered up, "Hey, Jack and I have some questions. Can you come down and answer a few?"

Bishop knew he would; it was a matter of if he could right then or not. He didn't receive an immediate verbal answer but heard his dad get up and move toward him.

"Yes, I have some time right now, so let's do it. I'm going to grab a drink. You boys want anything?"

Bishop grinned as he saw his father round the staircase and head down. "Nah, Jack and I just finished a snack, so we're good."

Greg grabbed a drink and headed to the living room couch. "Come on in here, guys. Bring the papers you have."

In just a minute or so, Jack, Bishop, and Sophie were all on the sectional sofa looking at Greg.

"So tell me about your questions, and let me see how I can help."

Now that they had someone to ask, the boys had no idea on how to get started!

"Dad, Jack asked if the same Talent was passed down from one generation to the next. Like, if his mom is a Finder, is he likely to be a Finder too?"

Bishop and Jack were glancing at each other, anxious to have some answers.

Greg leaned back further into the couch and set his drink on the side table.

"Ohhh! Coaster, Mr. B!" Jack said urgently.

He had been caught more than once with no coaster, and apparently, that was a mortal sin according to Ellen. Greg's eyes widened as he snatched his drink off the table, wiped the wet spot, grabbed a coaster from the stack, and carefully placed his drink on it.

"Now that I owe you my life"—Greg chuckled—"how can I help you again?"

Jack laughed and said, "DNA, dude. DNA."

"Right! Okay, yes, genetics play a part in all this as it does seem to be something that is passed down in the family lines. There do seem to be some connections between gifts the parents have and gifts their children may have. Ellen and myself have no defined Talent, but Bishop here is supposed to be an Omni. We have a Knower in the family, and she was able to tell us that much."

"So I will likely be a Finder like my mom?" Jack sounded dubious about this Talent as he has seen some on the list he liked better.

"It's likely but not necessarily true. It *tends* to be true, but again, not always," said Greg.

Jack grimaced as he faced the prospect of what he considered a boring Talent.

Bishop could tell Jack was not well pleased with this information, so he tried another question. "So, if it's generally tied to genetics, Jack could find out what Talents other people in his family have had, and he might get those instead, right?"

Greg leaned forward as he answered, "Exactly correct. It is proven there is a genetic component, but Joan is not the sole genetic contributor to Jack. It could be another Talent that is in the family line that pops into play. Just like in families that have all brown eyes, and one pops in with a green or blue eyes instead. It doesn't have to be parent to child. I mean, again, look at Bishop. Ellen and I have no specific Talent, but he will be an Omni."

Jack's face brightened at this thought. "So, I really need to talk to Mom about our family tree and look at some of the Talents that pop up!"

Bishop was keenly interested in familial Talent as well now. "Do we have a family tree that would give me some of that information too? I'd really like to see what kinds of Talent we have had and have an idea of what my three Talents may be."

Greg nodded and said, "Ellen has quite a bit of that mapped out. It's pretty incomplete. Not everyone wanted to admit to Talent through the years, and not everyone had the understanding about Talent we do today. You'll have to get that from her when she gets home later. Did you have any more questions?"

Bishop didn't and was about to get up when Jack started talking, "So every family has a list of these Talents and has kept a family tree, right?"

Greg frowned. "No, that has not always been true. Again, people could be frightened by this and hide it or not realize they had a Talent and not even mention it. If you knew nothing about Talent yet you were always able to find what you were looking for, would you realize you were a Finder? Probably not, and that is true in history as well. It is quite possible all Talent was not recorded in a family line. The list of Talent we have has been expanded and updated through the years based on our family and friends. Things we found to be false were removed, and things we found to be true were added."

Both boys looked at each other in silence for a minute. Greg got up and excused himself as soon as they began to talk to each other. It was clear they didn't need his input any longer.

"Sophie wants to go for a walk. Let's head down to the park and let her play for a while."

Bishop headed back to the kitchen to get her harness and leash while Jack followed behind, and they headed out to the park.

As they approached the park, they realized it was not going to be the location for any deep discussions. Small children ran like herds of rats through the park, yelling, playing, and in the middle of everything. There was a small circle of moms under the pavilion occasionally shouting out, "You better stop that! You wanna go home now? Bet that hurt, didn't it! Rub some dirt on it. You're fine!"

Bishop absently walked over to the dog area and went inside. Although less crowded, it was also in the brutal Texas sun. This was not the location to sit and chat. When Sophie was done, they headed back and began talking as they had on the way down.

"I'm not patient enough for this," Jack announced. "Now that I know I may have a Talent, I want to know what it is, and I'm worried it will be something lame, like being a Finder!"

Bishop wanted to laugh, but he was too loyal to his friend for that. "You're just going to have to ask your mom about it. Only thing that might give you more answers."

Jack nodded absently in agreement.

As the boys returned to Bishop's house, Jack announced he was going home to talk to his mother.

"Hey, I'm going to head home for a bit and ask my mom some questions. I want to know what other talents there are and see what kind of information she can give me."

Bishop understood. "Yeah, Jack, holler or just come back when you're done," he said as he and Sophie veered into the driveway of his house.

He went in, tossed Sophie's harness and leash on the counter, and grabbed a soda. He wanted to know more, but also, he was feeling uneasy. He couldn't explain it, but he was. His mother still wasn't home. So he chugged his soda and left the can on the counter, and he and Sophie went upstairs. They laid across the bed as Bishop thought about all he had learned in the last few days. What days they had been! As he considered them, he fell asleep with Sophie curled up next to him.

CHAPTER 19

LESSONS IN HISTORY

Bishop had been eager for his mother to get home, until she did.

"Bishop Lincoln Brown, get your skinny butt down here and clean up!" Her voice from the bottom of the stairs filled his bedroom loudly enough to wake him up, cause him to jump, and almost fall off the bed altogether.

"I'm coming!" he yelled before she headed up the stairs to get him.

He looked around bewildered for a moment, glanced at Sophie who was sitting up looking at him now, and snapped his fingers as he walked to the door. They headed down the stairs to face his mother together.

"Are you blocking?"

The look on Bishop's face gave away the answer.

"Start blocking now! Also, look at this mess! Halter, leash, muffin wrappers, crushed cans, and a half-eaten bowl of popcorn? Are you serious? I suggest you clean all this up immediately. I'm going to my study."

"Mom," Bishop began, "I wanted to—"

"Bishop, I'm warning you. Clean this up. Then I will talk to you about whatever, but block and clean!"

Ellen stormed off, and Bishop looked at Sophie.

"I don't know, girl, when do *you* think the alien got her?" He chuckled at his own joke but stifled it quickly in case she was listening.

He did realize, now, that he had left quite a mess behind. It only took three minutes to clean, and then he was off to find his mom.

Ellen was watching him with a nasty side-eye as he walked up the steps to her study above the master bedroom.

"It's all cleaned up!" Bishop said with a grin.

"Are you blocking?" Ellen responded, still giving him a good bit of side-eye.

Bishop hung his head. He forgot one of the she things she gave him to do, and she didn't look like she was in the mood to play. He sat down on the floor where he was and just took a second. He found his heartbeat, felt it beating strongly, and began to follow it up, up, up to his head. The warm feeling was different than usual but not bad. He wondered why that was but, for now, pushed the thought back. He had bigger fish to fry.

"Sorry, Mom. I'm ready now," he said.

The side-eye dissolved into a brief chuckle from his mom.

"Okay, so what did you want to know now," she said as she turned her chair to face him.

"Well," began Bishop, "Jack and I were reading the list of Talents and had questions. Dad answered a lot of them, but some he said we'd have to ask you about."

Ellen nodded her head. "Okay, where's Jack then?"

"He went home to ask Joan questions about her family history to see what his DNA may hold as far as Talents."

Ellen paused and cocked her head to the side. "Okay, do we wait for him, or do we proceed?"

Bishop hadn't thought about waiting for Jack.

He figured Jack would be asking his mom the questions, so he said, "Let's just go ahead. I can catch Jack up if I need to. We wanted to each know about our family trees and what Talents may be in there. It would give me an idea of what Talents I may get. He's asking Joan, and I'm asking you!"

"Well then," she said, "let's begin. The tree is very incomplete. However, we can trace it back, we think, to the early 1200s in England. From what I've been able to find, even when some generations were 'skipped,' most public records were kept well enough for us to fill the gaps. I have nothing but names, birth dates, and deaths on a lot of people. On some, I don't have more than a name or who they married. It's not easy, but part of what I have done is more digging and checking relations to complete our family tree back further. The family tree is so extensive though that every Talent out there has cropped up at some time, so I don't know that it nails that down for you."

Bishop considered what she said. It was true if there was that much history, there would be no way to track the specific Talents he might have.

"Yeah, I guess that's too much history to narrow it down. Thanks for the information though."

"Yo! Bishop!" Jack's voice was unmistakable.

"In Mom's office!" Bishop yelled back.

Good thing his mom and dad weren't weird about having people in their study.

"What'd you find out when you talked to Joan?" Bishop asked.

Jack's look of frustration told Bishop he didn't get what he was hoping for, and Bishop wondered if he got any answers at all.

"Mom said she's a Finder, and that's all she knows. There's no family history of Talent that she knows of. I even asked about dad." Jack hung his head when he said it.

"Oh, Jack!" Ellen jumped in. "I'm sorry you weren't able to get the information you wanted. What exactly did your mom say about your dad?"

Jack just kept his head down and said, "Not much. He didn't have any Talent that she knew of, and that was it. She doesn't have a family tree and was never big into genealogy or whatever. I guess, if I have a Talent at all, I will be a Finder."

Nobody spoke for a minute, and then Bishop said, "That's not true. Based on what Mom and Dad have told me, just because your dad didn't know about it didn't mean he didn't have Talent, and more Talent could be on his side that was still passed down to you. I think you need to be ready to be anything!"

Jack looked up and grinned. "Yeah, that's right. I could still be something cool." He turned to look at Ellen and then told Bishop, "Mom sent me with snacks. Wanna go check them out?"

Ellen laughed as they barreled down the stairs shoving and yelling—just like two completely normal boys. Except that they weren't.

CHAPTER 20

FORGOTTEN ENVELOPE

Joan had indeed sent snacks; and as they were working their way through chicken salad sandwiches, chips, and lemonade, Jack asked, "So anything else specific your mom said that I missed?"

Bishop shook his head no as his mouth was too full for a verbal response.

"Okay, did you ever look at the Manila envelope Mr. Molina gave you?"

Bishop's eyes bulged, he had completely forgotten about it. There had been so much! He shook his head no again but also put his finger to his overfull lips to remind Jack they had told no one yet. They doubled down on eating and finished their snack in no time. Once done, they headed upstairs with Sophie in tow.

"I read one letter from Mr. Molina," Bishop said as they opened the Manila envelope, "but that's it. Here, this is the one."

He passed the letter from Mr. Molina to Jack.

Jack read it quickly and said, "Wow!" and then asked a question that made Bishop feel pretty dumb. "So where's the Prophecy he's talking about?"

"I don't know. I really didn't have time to look through it last time, and then I had forgotten!"

Unlike his grandfather's letters, these were often photocopies and had a translation attached. They split the pile to try to find something that looked like a prophecy. It wasn't easy. There were a lot of letters; plus, they didn't know exactly what they were looking for. No letter said "prophecy" on the outside of it.

"Bro, we should focus on the ones we can read first and then muddle through the others if we can't find it."

Jack's idea had merit, and Bishop was glad he thought of it. Each of their piles then turned into two piles. One pile was "with translation" and one pile was "please don't let the Prophecy be in this one." Two boys plus four piles was too much for Bishop's bed; Bishop slid off the bed and dragged his chair over to one side with his two piles, leaving Jack plenty of room to navigate his piles while sitting on the bed.

Jack began to read part of a letter out loud, "'I am an Influencer, and my mother was a Sorcerer. I am the last of my line. But my brother Ferdinand has children, and his may see Talent.' Do you remember an Influencer being on your mom's list?"

Bishop didn't have the list anymore but was fairly certain that wasn't listed.

"No, but remember what Dad said about things that were changed through the years? An Influencer may have become something else over time. That copy looks like the actual letter is a billion years old. Maybe it's called something else now. Plus, Mom's list talked about what people assumed the Talents were. An Influencer and a Sorcerer could be completely different things on Mom's list now. We should ask her for a copy of it to keep."

Jack nodded and they continued to read.

Bishop found an interesting section and read it out loud, "This says, 'I am a Sorcerer. I store my magic in my stone. It is available for my use at any time.' Maybe that's what Mom's list calls a Sourcer, and they are calling a Sorcerer?"

Jack's nod went unseen as he said, "Yeah, seems legit. Besides, Mr. Molina's papers are sure to be different from yours because they are supposed to be from different sides. I'm sure they didn't communicate much."

This time, Bishop's nod went unseen as both boys continued to search through the letters.

"Oh! Bishop! This may be it!" Jack had a letter open but was pointing to the end of the page. "When the present unites with the past, true peace shall emerge. One who is fair. One who is strong. One who has mastered the Talents. This shall remove the evil and wrong. This shall unite the House."

The boys looked at each other. It looked like the Prophecy had been found, and if Bishop was the One, there was a lot of responsibility lying on his shoulders. He had to be fair, strong, and master the Talents; and then he had to remove evil and wrong and then unite the House. It didn't sound possible.

"Jack, I can't be the One. There's no way I could ever do all this!" Bishop began to panic.

"Bro, they *think* you're the One. Do your best. If you can't do it, then it was never you. They'll find another 'One.'"

Jack's pragmatic take on this was a relief to Bishop. Maybe, just maybe, his laissez-faire approach to life wasn't all bad. Try and try hard, but if it's not him, it never was. What a great way to look at this!

ABOUT THE AUTHOR

Sheridan is from Texas and began writing stories when she began writing. Her love of words and storytelling are legendary in her family—especially during long road trips! Her love of reading led to her continue this as a lifelong hobby. She spent twenty years in education before moving to the job of her dreams: writing and working in publishing. "Do what ya gotta, then do what ya love."